THE RUNAWAY HUSBAND

very witty mystery fiction

JULIE HIGHMORE

Published by The Book Folks

London, 2023

ISBN 978-1-80462-087-8

www.thebookfolks.com

THE RUNAWAY HUSBAND is the second standalone
mystery in the EDIE FOX DETECTIVE AGENCY series
by Julie Highmore. Look out for the first,
THE MISSING AMERICAN. More details can be
found at the back of this book.

For Carol

ONE

I was sitting on Brighton beach during the first week of September, willing the heatwave to end.

'Just two more pebbles,' I told Alfie, desperate to leave and find shade. He was throwing them into the sea, or attempting to. He was so rubbish at it that some ended up behind him. I'd google five-year-olds' throwing skills when I got back.

'Ouow,' moaned Alfie. 'Not two pebbles. More!'

'How many, then?'

He opened his palm and pointed at fingers, whispering as he counted. 'Twenty-fourteen?' he asked, all liquid-brown eyes in a halo of dark curls. Alfie was no prodigy, but he was always the cutest kid wherever we went. How sorry I felt for other grandparents.

'And then we can leave?' I asked.

As he ignored me, our dog sniffed around a topless woman and her fully clothed male friend, the smell of their warm pizza having drifted our way.

'Bear!' I yelled, realising too late that it sounded like 'Bare!'

'Cool dog,' said the woman, lobbing a crust his way.

'Thanks.' I pointed at the sea and said to Bear, 'Swim!'

The massively wet and hairy Portuguese water dog my daughter had paid a small fortune for galloped back into the waves to rejoin Alfie's game, snapping at the flying pebbles without actually catching one and cracking a tooth. Bear was nowhere near as dumb as he looked.

While I was checking the weather forecast on my phone, hoping for a cold snap, it rang. It was my partner in crime, Mike, calling from Oxford.

'Hey, Edie. How's things?'

'Hot,' I told him. 'That's how they are.'

'Same here. Great, isn't it?'

'No!'

He laughed. 'Oh, yeah. Forgot.'

Early summer, I'd bought a mini freezer for the office and packed it with ice cubes. With its door open wide and a fan beside it, we had air conditioning, of sorts.

'I should move to Lapland,' I said.

'No, don't do that. Well, not yet.'

'Oh?'

'Are you sitting down?'

'Er, yeah.' My mind shot to a dark place. Had the office burned down, or was it my house?

'Looks like Fox Wilder might have a case,' said Mike. 'Like, a real one.'

'Really?'

We hadn't had anything at all for two months. It was as though adulterers and lost cats took the summer off. Luckily, we all had other sources of income. Emily – late twenties, school dropout, ex drug addict, and clever – studied part-time and worked in the shop beneath our office. Mike – mid-thirties – acted and tutored, and I project-managed my Oxford house refurb, kind of. Also, when not in Brighton grannying, I'd done quite a bit of supply teaching.

After the trauma of our first big case eighteen months ago, being back in the classroom, making tiny togas and getting seven-year-olds not to mumble the lines of their

Romans play had been good, comforting even. Unfortunate events had caused me to want to give up on the agency, but Mike had talked me into letting it toddle along, saying he'd put money in to expand, market etc., once he'd sold his house in Surrey. I'd tried telling him he was asking too much, but he wouldn't have it.

I tucked the phone under my chin, opened a bottle of water, and took a swig. 'Tell me more.'

'A woman called Jessica emailed saying she needs to find her husband, who's been missing for weeks. Said she'd tell us more tomorrow.'

Bear came bounding up, stopped two feet away, and shook lovely cold seawater over me, almost as though I'd trained him to do that. 'Interesting. And that's all she said?'

'Yep. I'll forward you her email.'

'It's OK, I'll have it on my phone. When's she coming in?'

'I haven't suggested a time yet.'

'If you make it late morning, I'll be there.'

'You sure?'

'Alfie's back at school tomorrow, so I could head home this evening.'

'That would be great.'

Alfie had managed to throw a pebble at his own cheek and ran towards me howling.

'Better go,' I told Mike. 'See you tomorrow.'

'Yeah, I'll let you know what time. Drive safely.'

'I'm sorry?' I said, but he'd gone. Were men ever told to drive safely?

Alfie sobbed beside me, so I kissed his sore spot better, part-dried the dog, packed everything into my rucksack, and took us to a beach café for two ice creams and a doggie bowl of water. While Alfie and I licked at rapidly melting cones, I wondered again why Brighton City Council hadn't thought of trees along the promenade.

My daughter's house – inherited from her father, who'd inherited it from his grandmother – was on the Hove end of Brighton. It was a grand-looking, terraced, four-storey, five-bedroomed Victorian affair that Terence had rented out for decades but apparently never visited. Luckily for me, it had a self-contained basement for visitors. It was all a bit dated, but that was how Maeve and her partner Jack liked it, and they'd changed very little since moving in, not even the tired William Morris wallpaper. 'I know you're going for hip minimalist in your little house, Mum,' Maeve had said, 'but if we did that here, it would be like living in Stansted Airport.'

I rather liked Stansted and would move in tomorrow, but saw what she meant. The other thing was, she and Jack had no time to even think about doing the place up.

On arriving in Brighton, they'd opened a vegan café near the train station, hoping to catch commuters. They'd combined their names to call it 'Jama's', which I thought conjured up sleepwear, not food. But as the sign had gone up, I kept my thoughts to myself. When it became clear, however, that hardly anyone wanted jackfruit for breakfast, they'd revamped the menu and changed the name to Maeve's Caff. Now they could barely keep up with the demand for bacon – outdoor-reared, organic – in a crusty roll.

Maeve could have gone back to her post-grad studies or been a full-time mother, so financially comfortable was she now, thanks to her dad. 'Yeah,' she'd said, when I brought it up, 'but Jack and I want to be part of the Brighton vibe. You know?' As someone who'd impulsively given up teaching to open a detective agency, I guessed I did know.

I let myself, Alfie, and the dog into the house, where Zachary – the latest nanny – whisked Alfie off for a bath while Bear lapped up more water after the saltiness of the English Channel. Jack was cooking something exotic-smelling, which I wished I could have stayed for, and Maeve was still at the café.

'I need to get back to Oxford,' I told Jack.

'That's a shame.' He stopped speed-chopping and looked up. 'Problem with the builders?'

'Not this time. It's a possible new case.'

'Oh?' he said, his eyes lighting up.

Jack had been my previous partner in crime, albeit briefly. I sensed he missed investigating, but since he was now committed to Maeve, Brighton, tossing bacon for a living, and being a stepdad to Alfie, he'd never have said so. Alfie's birth father was a fellow traveller Maeve had hooked up with during her post-grad gap year. He'd chosen not to acknowledge Alfie's existence, so I regularly thanked the universe for Jack.

'A woman called,' I said, 'wanting to find her husband.'

'And you don't feel you can leave it to Mike, Emily and Naz?'

'No Naz anymore.' Naz had been a hero during our first big case. 'Sadly, we lost him to Durham University a year ago.'

'Oh,' said Jack. 'I really haven't kept up.'

'Understandably.'

'Anyway, my going back is more like FOMO.'

Jack laughed. 'I get that.'

'And I should check on the house as well. Make sure the builder isn't creating rococo arches for the knocked-down walls.'

'Like ours, you mean?' He grinned and pointed at the one that extended their kitchen. 'Maybe they'll make a comeback. Like tiny mobile phones… and Rich Tea biscuits.'

'My favourites,' I said. 'Great dunkers. Listen, I'll call Maeve and explain.'

'Sorry you have to go,' said Jack.

'Yeah, me too.'

After packing up my things in the basement, loading them into the car, and blowing a kiss to Alfie through the middle bay window, I set off for home feeling little guilt. Alfie would be back at school the next day, and, besides, he had Zachary. And Maeve had Jack, and Jack had Maeve. Unless you counted my builder Gary, topping up his pension, I had no one waiting for me at home, if you could call it a home these days.

* * *

I was in Oxford by nine, despite delays passing Heathrow. I'd already texted Gary to warn him I'd be in the house when he and the others arrived the following morning, and the first thing I saw was a note he'd left. I braced myself. Gary had a way of making me feel I was responsible for any problems he encountered.

"Edie, your single skin scullery wall will NOT pass building regs if incorporated into new utility room", said this one, as though I'd personally laid the bricks and mortar in 1890. He had neat sloping handwriting that brought to mind my lovely, late, policeman dad's. "You'd best put a stud wall off the single skin with plaster and skim."

How quiet the house was, and, when I dropped my bag on the floor, echoey. I picked up an oil-covered Biro and wrote, "Thanks, Gary, will get going on it ASAP!" I drew a laughing emoji, in case he really would leave that job for me, made my way past RSJ props and drills, and Daily Star newspapers, hammers and wrenches, tubs of screws, and hanging sheets of plastic, until I reached the temporary kitchen area and the kettle.

I desperately wanted a cup of tea, but found everything covered in a fine layer of brown chalk, including the kettle. It looked dangerous, and I felt my eyes sting, and not just from toxic dust.

I blinked hard and tried to stay positive.

Making tea wasn't an option, and I was too tired and bedraggled to walk to a café, so I took a bottle of pinot grigio from the fridge, then emptied my favourite mug of cigarette butts and gave it a good soapy wash.

Thankfully, the guys hadn't reached the bedrooms yet, although they'd been scheduled to repaint them weeks ago. I went through another plastic screen and hauled two bags up the stairs – the mug handle between my teeth, the icy bottle under my arm. This floor was still recognisable, thank God. When downstairs, I could barely work out where everything had once been, and often referred to the photos I'd taken before the team had arrived.

Originally, aeons ago, it had been me, my sister, and my baby living here; then me and my child for twenty-two years; then me, my child, and her child for almost four. Now it was time for a new start, or at least a new phase.

Lucky me, I told myself as I mounted the stairs, free to please myself for a few weeks. Free to enjoy a cooling shower, a glass of wine, and an episode of my latest binge watch in this empty, half-destroyed house with no one else in it. Not Maeve. Not Alfie. Not even the cat, who'd also buggered off to Brighton. I reached my nice, neat bedroom with its king-sized empty bed, just waiting for lucky me.

TWO

I was wrenched from sleep at half seven when the drilling began and the bed shook. My heart raced until I remembered where I was and what was going on. Sitting up and yawning, I could even feel my ribs vibrating. Perhaps, I thought, once I'd met this Jessica and set the others to work on the case, I'd drive back to Brighton and stay until Gary had taken his concrete mixer, and his hammers and drills and Radio Oxford on to the next client.

No, I couldn't do that. There were kitchen cupboards to choose, along with wood flooring. 'You've got your walnut, oak, ash…' Gary had said on the phone. 'Solid wood or engineered flooring. Then there's laminate. Good as the real thing these days. And you might want to think about coordinating your flooring with your kitchen units, your wall tiles, and your splashbacks. You don't want no mishmash like you had before.'

I had no idea where to start, despite the stack of catalogues gathering chalk and sawdust on what used to be our kitchen table. I'd tried closing my eyes and manifesting a TV company swooping in and taking over, or less feasibly, my stylish friend Astrid offering to help.

No, I was stuck in Oxford for at least a week, and as I lay back with fingers in ears, watching the ceiling light tremble and the wicker chair shuffle my way, I formed a plan: shower, get dressed, take laptop to café, eat breakfast, google temporary accommodation, meet the potential new client.

It was a beautiful morning on the Cowley Road, just around the corner from my house. The diverse and student-filled area was as vibrantly edgy as Oxford could manage. It was a stone's throw from the dreaming spires and cloisters of the city centre, but strictly off limits to tourists, or rather, off their maps. Occasionally, a visitor unwittingly crossed the invisible Magdalen Bridge barrier, looking bewildered and trying to find Hogwarts.

The students know the area though, with many of them, from both Oxford and Brookes universities, living in shared houses in Victorian side streets or student blocks on nearby St Clements. They'd be back towards the end of September, but for now all was relatively quiet, and, with no queuing or waiting, a person could grab anything from a traditional full English breakfast to a Middle Eastern quinoa, feta, and pomegranate salad at half nine in the morning. I went for the former.

* * *

Our prospective client looked as cool as Audrey Hepburn at her coolest when she stepped through the office door and said, 'Oh, hello. Am I in the right place? Fox Wilder? Private investigators?'

She was early to mid-forties, slim, and around five-seven, with sleek dark hair that swept across her sunglasses and ended in a small upward flick on her shoulders. Her lemon linen dress was sleeveless and knee-length and made for someone, like her, with no lumps. She wore peachy lipstick, a solid gold bangle with matching earrings, and soft flat pumps a shade darker than the dress.

She shook my hot hand with her cool one and said, 'Jessica Relish.'

As she took a seat, I gave her a welcoming smile. 'My sister's Jessica, but prefers Jess. What do you like to—'

'Oh, Jessica. Please.'

Only one person had ever abbreviated my name. *My Little Eed*, my dad had called me for years, before first dropping the 'My', then the 'Little'.

'I'm Edie,' I told Jessica, 'and this is Emily.'

Jessica took in long-legged Emily with her pink-streaked fair hair, phone at the ready. 'You're not recording me, I hope?'

'Emily finds it quicker to take notes on her phone.'

'Ah.' Jessica shook her head. 'The young never fail to impress me. I have twin sons, whom I swear someone switched with cyber geniuses aged six.' She laughed. 'They were so adorably human up to that point.'

'Aw,' said Emily, pulling a poor-you face. 'Actually, I'm twenty-seven. Not that young.'

'Gosh, you don't look it.'

'Thanks.'

'So,' I said, opening my notepad and clicking my pen, 'how can we help you, Jessica?'

By 'we' I meant not just Emily and me, but also Mike Wilder, who was listening in on the other side of a slightly open sliding door. He often went undercover, so it was important that he wasn't seen.

Jessica propped the sunglasses on her head, tucking her hair back and revealing a flawless complexion and perfect eyebrows. 'I can't find my husband, Hugh. Hugh Horsfield.'

'OK.' I wrote down the name.

'I want to serve him divorce papers, but have no idea where he is. The last I heard, he was shacking up with his girlfriend, Zara, in Summertown. I've tried calling, obviously, but his phone was cut off when I stopped paying for it, a month or so ago. For a while, he used someone's else's pay-as-you-go, non-smartphone, and we spoke once or twice, mainly about the boys. But that one went dead three weeks ago. Although I managed to find a mobile number for Zara, I haven't called her.'

'Why not?' I asked.

'I was worried it would alert her, and therefore him. Also, deep down, I thought... Hugh always came home, you see. Until now.'

'He's had other affairs?'

'Numerous, although I'm not sure they'd count as affairs. Tracking down a Tinder babe from her boobs and arse alone would have been impossible, but this one's different. Now I have a face and name and place of work. Until he gets in touch with me, I fear only Zara can lead me, or hopefully you guys, to him.'

'Unless he's dumped her?' said Emily.

'That had occurred to me. But since I cut off all financial assistance, Hugh's only bank account has seen no activity. Somebody's helping him, giving him cash. I feel sure it's still Zara, but I could be wrong.'

I thought of Mike, holed up and possibly wanting to sneeze in the next room. 'There's a café next door with much better coffee than we can offer. Shall we continue in there?'

'Sure,' said Jessica, reaching for a very nice grey satchel.

I took a pro forma contract from my desk drawer for her to sign in the café. Judging from her outfit, I'd be quoting our highest hourly rate.

Next door, we quickly put our drinks and cakes on the last free table, and Emily got her phone out again to take notes.

'I was married once before,' Jessica told us over her flat white. 'To Derek. He was older. We had twin boys, William and Harry... yes, I know, but he'd insisted. I've always called them Will and Hal, and as far as I can tell, they haven't been traumatised by their royal names. When we divorced, Derek helped me set up the hospitality business. I changed my name to make it easier to run a company called Jessica Relish. Derek kindly let me keep the family home in Primrose Hill. He was very good to me, but mostly out of guilt. He'd met and fallen for the hearty and straightforward Pippa, the exact opposite of me, according to the twins.'

'How old are the boys?' asked Emily.

'They're about to turn fifteen. Almost out of the surly early-teen stage. They see their father occasionally. More, in fact, since Hugh's disappearance, although they absolutely adore Hugh. He's always such fun with them. With everyone, really. The life and soul... you know the type. And with no proper job of his own, he's been indispensable to me at home. I have franchises scattered around the UK, so I'm away a lot.'

'Sounds exciting,' said Emily.

Jessica smiled at her. 'It's exhausting, but fun. Anyway, I met Hugh ten years ago, when I catered for a graduation party that his parents threw here in Oxford. I was thirty-nine and newly divorced. Hugh was twenty-two. Everyone said, "It won't last!" and of course they've turned out to be right. Unless he does come home, of course. Change his ways. Anyway, it was love at first sight for both of us. All that corny eyes-across-a-crowded-room, the thunderbolt, the butterflies, the feeling that we'd known each other before.'

'Like in another life?' asked Emily.

'Who knows? I just remember that instant recognition, the very physical shock I experienced on meeting him. He was beautiful, and he thought I was too, and… well, we tried to have a relationship, but he was all over the place. Not such a wonderful dad substitute back then. He dropped out of an MBA in London, visited his mates all over the world, and tried to be a novelist. As far as I could tell, he was screwing everything with a heartbeat. In the end his parents cut off all funds, and around the same time, I found myself pregnant.'

'Oh,' said Emily. 'So you have another…'

'I lost it at sixteen weeks. We'd just had a speedy marriage because Hugh had wanted to be a proper father. Nothing at all to do with his parental allowance being cut off and my growing business, ha ha.'

'I'm sorry to hear about the miscarriage,' said Emily.

'Thanks,' said Jessica. 'Hugh was devasted by it, but we kept trying for another, which was fun, I have to say. All was going well until I discovered evidence of Hugh seeing other women. I confronted him, he apologised, and said they'd meant nothing and that he'd never do it again, blah, blah. Instead of kicking him out – thinking of the boys – I insisted on him agreeing to a postnup agreement. I mean, obviously, I still loved him too.'

'Postnup?' I asked.

'They're newish, but increasingly popular. The bottom line was that if Hugh strayed again, it would mean instant divorce proceedings and a settlement for him of only fifty thousand pounds. Postnups can be difficult to enforce, but I don't think Hugh knows that.' Jessica took a chunk of one of the two cakes Emily had cut into three and nibbled daintily as she spoke. 'Before my accident, which I'll fill you in on later, Hugh had taken to going away overnight again to see old uni mates I hadn't heard of. Or, if I was working away, he'd go out for dinner with some friend or relative who just happened to be in London. He'd get Pat our cleaner to sit with the boys. Sorry, am I going too fast?'

'No,' said Emily, tapping away on her phone. 'I've developed this, like, shorthand system?'

'You're doing fine,' I said. All I'd written was "Tinder Dinners Pat".

Jessica took a sip of water. 'It was déjà vu all over again, sadly, and whenever I asked what the hell he was up to, he'd gaslight me. He called me paranoid and even got some random guys to message me confirming they'd met up with him on the dates in question. It was all a bit tragic, you know? The older wife coming across as insecure. I hated it, that feeling of rejection again.'

'You mean because your first husband left you?'

'Lord, no. I rather engineered that one myself, although the boys must never know.'

'Ah.'

'I meant previous rejection by Hugh. There was also my father, of course, but since I'm not paying you to psychoanalyse me...' Jessica took another sip of the water Emily had fetched for us all. Her hand shook slightly when she put the glass down. 'So, yes, I had my suspicions, but then Hugh did his usual thing. He became super attentive and sweet again, and I convinced myself he adored only me. I also concluded that he was still young and so needed to socialise with people his own age, and as the boys had become more independent, he should be free to see his friends.' She picked up her glass but put it down again. 'However...'

'Yes?'

'Deep down? I knew.'

'Right.'

'And so I checked his phone. Hugh is massively charismatic, but as is often the way with that type, he's careless. Or cavalier. Both. He uses the same pin numbers, passcodes and passwords for everything, and although he regularly deletes entire email and text threads, he also uses mobile banking, in which you can't, as far as I know, delete transactions. He regularly left his phone lying around, and of course I knew his passcode. Whenever I checked his account, I noticed more and more purchases occurring in Oxford. These happened at times we weren't there, or rather here, together, staying in the flat that Hugh's parents had bought for him, which is now in my name. It's not far from here, about halfway up Divinity Road. Couldn't believe my luck when I walked past the shop and saw your plaque.'

'What kind of purchases?' I asked.

'Oh, um, cinema tickets? Meals out? Ann Summers…'

'Eew,' Emily said, and tapped away.

'From what I'd seen on his phone, I guessed he was seeing one particular person, rather than screwing around, and that she lived in Oxford.'

'Right.' I thought back to Greg and that sick feeling I'd get when I found yet another name and number in his phone or scribbled on a scrap of paper. Often, they were just an unsubtle initial.

'Basically, Hugh and I were not in a good place, but we continued as though we were, mainly for the boys' sake. I suppose I turned a blind eye and got on with my life and my job while I thought about what to do.'

I jotted down, "Blind eye". It followed "Cavalier". I almost had a haiku. 'And did you decide what you were going to do?'

'Sort of. We hadn't been to Oxford for a while, although Hugh clearly had. So, a week before my accident, I fabricated a meeting in Oxford and suggested we stay in the flat. Hugh was keen, no surprise there. I suspected that he'd try to hook up with whoever he was seeing, so when I was supposedly meeting the client, I sat in a Cowley Road café and tracked his phone.

'Cool,' said Emily. 'Had you set him up in a "find my" app without him knowing?'

'I had. He'd no idea he'd approved it, poor lamb. I can't feel bad, though. If Hugh's brains hadn't been permanently in his boxers, and if he hadn't had so many silly gaming apps on his screen, he'd have noticed far earlier than he did. Which is another story.'

'And where did he go?' I asked.

'He first went to Headington, then to Summertown in north Oxford, where he parked for an hour and a half. I guessed Headington was where he met her, whoever, and then they went to her place in Summertown, or perhaps a hotel, before he drove home. This was all speculation at that point, obviously. Anyway, I left him enough time for a shower, then went back to the flat and told him the meeting had gone well. When I asked what he'd been doing, he said he'd gone for a run around South Parks, up at the top of Divinity Road.'

All three of us shook our heads and reached for cake.

'Anyway,' continued Jessica, 'my plan for the following week, when we returned to Oxford, was to have more fake meetings in the area and to somehow check out where Hugh had gone in Headington. From where the tracker had him parked, I guessed it was one of two cafés.'

'And what happened the following week?' I asked.

Jessica took a deep breath. 'Well... I felt sure Hugh wasn't going out for petrol, as he'd claimed that afternoon. The tank was three-quarters full. Careless Hugh again. And I wasn't cycling down Divinity Road to shop for a smart top in town, as I'd claimed. I wanted Hugh to think I was safely out of the way in the city centre, when, in fact, I was going to park the bike on Cowley Road and call for a taxi to take me to Headington. Once there, I'd simply look out for our car and watch nearby places, cafés and so on. I had no plan to confront Hugh, and a tiny part of me still thought it was all innocent. But when cycling down steep Divinity Road, my brakes wouldn't work properly. That's about all I remember, because the next thing I knew, I was in a coma and hearing voices.'

'Blimey,' I said. 'Were you badly hurt?'

'Apparently. There was some intercranial pressure and a suspected punctured lung, owing to broken ribs. They began to operate, but my blood pressure plummeted. I may have had a reaction to the anaesthetic, one doctor told me. I sort of remember leaving my body at one point. Surreal.'

'Yeah,' said Emily, 'it's so nice when that happens.'

I cleared my throat at her.

'I mean, er, like, all those people on YouTube who've had a near-death experience? They all say that.'

'Anyway,' continued Jessica, 'they felt they had no choice but to put me into a drug-induced coma. It was over two weeks before I began to come out of it. I still had a severe distal radius fracture, if that means anything to you?'

'A broken wrist?' asked Emily.

'Yes. I'm impressed!'

'Did that to both of mine, one time,' Emily added.

'Goodness,' said Jessica. 'How did you manage that?'

'Skiing accident,' I said quickly. She'd actually been off her head and tripped in the street. 'Didn't you ski into a tree?'

'Oh, right.' Emily pulled a sad face at Jessica. 'I did.'

Before Jessica could ask anything more, I jumped in again. 'So, were there other injuries?'

'I'd somehow developed an infection.'

'That's hospitals for you,' said Emily.

Jessica nodded. 'So, to cut to the chase, it was while I was in a coma that I found out the girlfriend's name was Zara and she ran a café in Headington.'

'How come?' I asked.

'Heard the two of them. And others, too, occasionally. Just bits and pieces. It was like everyone was talking underwater or on a not-quite-tuned-in radio.'

'That wasn't very clever of Hugh,' I said.

Jessica snorted. 'As I said, cavalier. After I was discharged, we went back to London and I convalesced while running the business from home, or trying to. I do have a fabulous PA, Ross. He's indispensable.'

"PA Ross", I wrote and added a question mark.

Jessica saw it and sniggered. 'Before you jump to conclusions, he's twenty-three. A little young, even for me.'

* * *

Back at the office, with a few more pages of notes and Jessica all signed up and paid up, Emily and I filled Mike in on what she'd told us, then randomly expressed what came into our heads.

'Aged forty-nine.'

'Can you believe that?'

No, we couldn't.

'Degree in Hospitality Business Management.'

'Met her first husband Derek in her early thirties. He was older and not a looker, but rich.'

'Twin boys, William and Harry, now aged fifteen, almost.'

'It's just plain cruel, naming them that.'

'Big house Primrose Hill, and a pied-à-terre in Oxford.'

'Divinity Road.'

'Love at first sight with Hugh.'

'I'm not sure I believe in love at first sight.' That was me. 'Thunderbolts and butterflies, eyes across a crowded room and instant recognition. I mean, does that actually ever happen?'

Emily shook her head. 'I don't believe in it either.'

'I believe in lust at first sight,' said Mike. 'Get struck by that once, twice a week. How about you guys?'

I stayed quiet, remembering this was a business meeting.

'That never used to happen to me,' said Emily. 'I reckon I can put it down to the ketamine, though. You know, sometimes I didn't even feel like my entire arms and legs for days?'

Mike and I exchanged looks of horror.

'Only now I'm with Ben, it's like amazing when we–'

'La, la, la,' I sang, putting my fingers in my ears. As clever as she was, Emily thought she was the first person ever to have had sex.

She hooted at me. 'You're so funny, Edie.'

'So,' said Mike, 'after having his funds cut off by Mummy and Daddy, Hugh jumped on the Relish gravy train by marrying Jessica.'

'He really should've changed his name to Relish,' said Emily.

'Why?' asked Mike.

'Hugh Horsfield?' I mean…' For some reason she and I got a fit of the giggles.

'Hugh Relish is worse. Sounds like a gay porn star.'

'I wouldn't know,' said Emily, our giggles subsiding. She tapped and scrolled on the new phone I'd bought her. She'd already typed up her notes and they were sitting neatly in the cloud she nagged us to use. 'I loved the postnup thing.'

'I thought it was a bit harsh,' said Mike.

'What?' I cried. 'After all she'd put up with?'

'I reckon she stayed because she fancied the pants off him,' said Emily. 'I'm not surprised, seeing the photo she showed us. Hugh's hot.'

'A bit too *Love Island*,' I said. 'Bland-looking, all muscle.'

'Exactly!'

I pulled a 'meh' face, and Emily laughed at me. Again. Then she left to do a shift in the shop downstairs. Her brother Oscar managed it and had given his sister her first proper job, post her rehab.

Mike had two hours to kill before teaching English Lit, one to one. He now only did the occasional bit-part acting and extras work. Mid-thirties, and knowing he'd never hit stardom, he was discovering how lucrative private tutoring could be, while occasionally going undercover fed his acting pangs. He seemed happy.

I jumped at his offer to drive me to the hotel I'd booked earlier, up on the business park. I really didn't want to take my car, since they charged guests for parking, plus there was a perfectly good bus stop close by.

We went back to my house and I battled my way through men and machines. Upstairs, I packed two cases: one just for clothes, the other for electronic items, washbag, books, and a bottle of red. Before going down to Mike waiting outside, I saw the folly of mixing liquid and laptop, so took out the bottle, downed some, and left the rest behind.

'We could take your bike too?' Mike said, throwing my bags on the back seat of his four-wheel drive. 'Put it on the rack?'

I hadn't ridden it in a while, Oxford being a city of drivers who hate cyclists. But then I thought it might be good for my health. Not that it had been great for Jessica's.

'No, I'm OK,' I said.

Once I'd crossed my fingers and assured Gary I'd almost finished coordinating fittings and flooring, we set off up the Cowley Road in Mike's beautifully air-conditioned monster of a vehicle, which, if he hadn't needed it, I'd have paid to camp in for a week.

THREE

The hotel was everything I'd expected, and more – more spacious, more corporate. Surfaces gleamed and staff members beamed. The fully stocked foyer bar twinkled enticingly, so after checking in, I dispatched Mike with a request for a margarita in twenty minutes and took my things up to room 235.

After a quick shower, I changed into something more appropriate than the denim shorts and vest I'd thrown on in the heat of my house. I went for a blue-grey, soft-cotton, cap-sleeved dress that I'd packed just in case I decided to eat in the restaurant. I found matching silver earrings and a bracelet, then slipped on strappy sandals with a bit of a wedge. Lipstick? Why not?

I blew Gary's dust off my best leather shoulder bag and transferred my notes and essentials to it. With my hair dry and shiny with hotel conditioner, I took a look in the long mirror and congratulated myself. I wasn't Jessica Relish, but I might have passed for her dirty-blonde and less thin older cousin.

Down in the bar, I spotted Mike at a table with my waiting cocktail. He watched me approach, then slapped a hand on the seat beside him. 'I'm sorry,' he said. 'I'm keeping this for a friend.'

'Oh, ha ha.'

He did a cartoon eye-rub with his knuckles. 'Edie?'

'I thought you were a good actor?' I said, sitting down.

'And I thought you were an east-Oxford boho?'

'Well…' I raised my glass carefully, so as not to spill a single drop. It was a perfect margarita – cold and sweet and salty. 'When in Rome.'

Mike took a swig of beer, then licked his top lip. While I'd been in Brighton, he'd closely shaved his head and sideburns, and, unlike me, the heat had turned him a healthy shade. Summer obviously suited him, and since he'd become a gym fanatic, it was hard to reconcile this scalped, toned, and chiselled Mike with the flabby one who'd appeared in the office almost two years ago pretending to be a clean-cut American. Today he could have passed for a bouncer or hitman.

'So, she wasn't wearing a cycle helmet?' he asked.

We seemed to be back on Jessica. 'Uh, no. She was only going to the Cowley Road so didn't bother.'

'Makes you think, doesn't it?'

'About getting your bike brakes checked?'

'About life. The small risks we take and get away with. Then one day, wham, you're in a coma.'

'It does.' I took another risky sip of the full cocktail, then another, and felt margarita splash on my hand.

'Steady on, Edie. You all right? Tell you what, why don't I order us some coffees?'

Was I all right? My head was swimming a bit. The heat, that wine earlier...

'Good idea,' I told him, and after the waitress had taken the order, along with my room number, I drained my glass and successfully landed it on the table.

Over coffee, we discussed Jessica's injuries.

'Lucky she didn't suffer permanent brain damage,' said Mike. 'I guess we could start by locating Zara and following her?'

'We could. But let's have a think first. Do a bit of research on Jessica, Zara and Hugh. Perhaps meet up tomorrow with Emily and take it from there?'

'OK.' Mike finished his beer. 'I'd better go and teach. Need a pee first, though.'

'Where are the loos?' I asked when he returned.

'Just over there, around the corner. I'll have to head off in five minutes, but I'll wait till you're back.'

'Cheers. Shall we say two o'clock at the office tomorrow? I think Emily's doing the late afternoon shift in the shop.'

'OK, I'll text her now.'

I picked up my bag and phone, and as I walked, I looked through the pictures that had been pinging in from Maeve. Alfie standing on a chair by the cooker, wearing his pyjamas and stirring the contents of a saucepan with a wooden spoon. "Jack's influence!" she'd written. There was also a video of Alfie on the beach after school with Zachary and Bear. "Great pebble throwing!"

I tried not to feel jealous as I looked up, spotted the loo, and pushed open the door. What I saw confused me. A row of strange sinks and the back of a man peeing into one? How disgust–

No, not sinks. Urinals.

'Oh, God, sorry!' I said, stupidly drawing attention to myself.

Flies were zipped up, and the man turned his head. The sun, pouring through the window behind, shrouded him in bright mistiness, but I could nevertheless see a big smile and amused eyes beneath his fair hair.

'Bit lost?' he asked.

I watched him saunter over to the basins and wash his hands. With soap. Straight back, square shoulders, just over medium height. Slim. Borderline skinny. My age? Late forties? He didn't bother with the dryer but shook water off as he approached me.

Two feet away, he stopped and stared, amused dark-brown eyes roaming over my face. This close to him, I saw his wavy hair was mostly grey, not blond. Grey with bits of brunette. Can a man be a brunette? Bit of a widow's peak. A vague beardy thing going on. Early fifties, I now thought. Not that I was thinking. My stomach was going bananas, and it was nothing to do with alcohol, or the heat, or bananas. What was this? He wasn't even that good-looking. Or was he? He had a lived-in face, but it was warm and actually quite lovely.

This was all wrong. I'd never liked beards… but this was a nice one, not even a beard really. Get a grip, I told myself. Move. Move your body. You've done it many times. I just needed to turn around, walk out the door, go and find the ladies. What a nice shirt, sleeves rolled back just enough. He had a familiar look. Or he resembled someone. That actor… used to be married to Angelina…

Billy Bob Thornton? As he is now. Or maybe ten years ago.

'I'm worried you'll get hit by the door,' he said. 'If someone comes in.'

He leaned past me to pull it open and I ducked under his arm.

'I'm sorry if I shocked you,' he said, out in the hallway. He went to put a hand on my shoulder but pulled back. No wedding ring.

'I must have shocked you too,' I said. I could still speak, that was good.

'You did, but in a very nice way.'

'I should go and find the person wearing a skirt.' I pointed at the male sign on the door beside us, deliberately using my left hand to show no wedding ring on me either. I may have left it hovering too long.

'Easy mistake to make,' he said, smiling. Nice voice. Deep. 'It's not like women don't wear trousers.' He glanced down and then up my dress, but not leerily. His mouth opened and then closed. What had he wanted to say? 'It's over there,' he told me, with a nod of the head.

'OK, thanks. Well, sorry again.'

It was a wrench, leaving this person, but Billy Bob was still there when I came out, leaning against the wall opposite, arms folded, head down, skinny legs crossed at the ankle. He clearly wasn't young, but at the same time seemed boyish.

He looked up, this time not smiling. 'I feel like I know you, although I'm sure we've never met.'

'I know,' I said with a nervous laugh.

'I wonder… this is crazy.' He rubbed his chin. 'I mean, are you…'

I relaxed, just a bit. At least the floor felt solid again.

'Here,' I said, finding a card in my bag pocket. He came over and took it.

'Edie,' he read. 'Pretty name.'

'Thanks.'

'I'm–'

'Call me?' I said. If he told me his name, I'd spend days looking him up. I also wanted to end this encounter on a high, not do or say something to trash myself. Leave the ball in his court. I pointed towards the bar. 'I should really get back to my partner.'

As I walked off, I heard a quiet, 'Oh.'

Having rounded the corner, I stopped and said, 'Shit.' I turned back. He was still standing there, tapping his hand with my card, and looking even better than five seconds ago.

'Business partner,' I called out, and he grinned, and I grinned, and then it really was time to get back to Mike.

Safe in my seat, I stared straight ahead, willing my eyes not to scan the bar and foyer.

'Are you all right?' Mike asked.

'Fine.'

'You sure?'

'Absolutely.'

He got up and slung his bag over his shoulder. 'Good. See you at two o'clock tomorrow, then.'

I thanked him for his help and waved him off, then finished my cold coffee and gathered my things. I made it to the lift. And then I made it to room 235. And as the door closed behind me, I leaned against it and my knees gave way, until I was sitting on the floor, propped against the door, feeling like a total teenager.

A text made a muffled ding inside my bag. How long had I been sitting there going over that brief encounter? Ten minutes? Two? I pulled my phone out and saw a text notification from a number I didn't recognise. I tapped it open.

"Where did you go?" it said.

'Oh, Jesus.' What to do, what to do. "Room 235", I replied before I could change my mind.

I sprang up and threw clothes back into my suitcase, along with *How to Stop Doubting Your Greatness and Start*

Living an Awesome Life from the bedside table. I checked my face in the mirror, reapplied lipstick, brushed my hair and sent a silent message to Maeve, apologising in advance if he turned out to be a strangler. Remembering John Steinbeck, I tugged him from my case and spread-eagled him on the bed.

Then I sat on the one chair, straight-backed and breathing slowly and deeply. In... calm... out... calm... in... What if I'd come across as a desperate middle-aged trollop? In... out... I checked my phone. Eleven minutes since I'd invited a total stranger to my room. He wasn't coming. I'd blown it. He definitely wasn't com–

The two knocks made me start, and when I opened the door, there he was waving a bottle of red.

'I thought we could use the toothbrush glasses?' he said, those brown Billy-Bob eyes penetrating my soul.

FOUR

While waiting in front of my half-Nordic friend Astrid's pristine front door, I examined the paintwork for chips and scratches. None. There were no smudges, or sticky finger marks, or signs that her five-year-old son had ever kicked the door with a muddy shoe. The original Edwardian tiles I was standing on were shiny and spotless, as were the door's glass panels. The small bay trees either side of the porch were entirely free of brown-edged leaves.

'Edie!' said Astrid, checking her watch. 'I'm afraid–'

I stepped into the hallway and passed her. It was best to be assertive, I'd learned. 'Just a quick hello,' I said. 'Shall I put the kettle on? Or have you got anything, you know, else?'

The watch was checked again and she sighed. 'Come. Studio.'

I'd have thought a wooden structure that housed garden tools, a mower, compost bin, and three bikes was a shed, but once stretched out on a recliner and halfway through the spliff she'd made me, I really didn't mind what Astrid called it.

Astrid was perched, all natural blonde and clear-skinned, on her tall stool beside her corner bench full of ceramics in progress, her pale-blue eyes penetrating the window, on the lookout for Milena. Astrid's cleaner was due any time, and Astrid really 'oughtn't', as she'd put it, 'frighten off another one'.

'So…?' she said, still staring at the house. Astrid was never one for eye contact, not unless she was very cross and forgot she didn't like it.

I had another puff on my spliff, as she puffed on hers. We never shared on account of the 'multiplying bacteria' that lips carry. Apparently.

'I've got a proposition for you,' I said bravely. 'Actually, a favour.'

'Would it involve a murderous, scheming ex of yours?'

She meant Terence, Maeve's dad. 'No, but thanks for the reminder.'

'Perhaps you need reminding, Edie. Before you fall for the next good-looking conman.'

'Huh!' I had planned to bring up Billy. 'He was Maeve's father, not some random stranger I'd picked up.'

Astrid's gaze turned to my vicinity, if not my face. 'I do worry about you, Edie.'

She didn't.

'OK,' I said, shifting my recliner more upright. 'I'm looking for someone to design my kitchen. You have a beautiful house, all put together by you, and so… Why are you laughing? Astrid, you never laugh.'

'I do when I'm stoned. Also when Jonathan gets amorous.'

Jonathan was Astrid's kind and lovely husband. They had an open marriage. Well, she did.

Astrid's laugh turned to a disbelieving smile. 'Have you any idea how much I'd charge, Edie? Considering you must be horribly leveraged, what with all the building work and your unsuccessful business. I mean, how could you afford me?'

I'd never told Astrid about the generous lump sum from my daughter, mainly because I wasn't stupid.

'Not a problem,' I said, with a dismissive wave. 'I've increased the mortgage to cover all the work.'

'Ha! I rest my case.'

'And,' I continued to fib, 'the agency is doing very well. Just got a big job. Wealthy client.'

'Ooh, do tell me more.' We were moving towards her comfort zone – logic, problem solving, giving sound advice. All of which I wished she'd apply to my kitchen, along with her artist's eye.

I told her about Jessica's accident.

'Who'd be crazy enough to cycle in Oxford?' she asked.

'Only millions of students.'

'Yes, but everyone makes allowances for them because they're so bloody dangerous themselves. All that one-handed weaving, holding a Tesco shop in the other.'

'Anyway,' I said, 'she ended up in a coma and heard her husband, Hugh, talking to his girlfriend in her hospital room. Once back home and recovering, she worked out who the woman was. Decided to divorce Hugh, but then couldn't find him to deliver the papers. The girlfriend, Zara, runs a café in Headington called, wait for it, Nice Buns.'

'Is that supposed to be funny?'

'I thought it was good.'

'Sounds like this Hugh is a bit dim. I mean, who doesn't know people in comas sometimes hear things?'

'Jessica described him as cavalier, but perhaps he didn't care. However, there was the postnup. You'd think he'd care about that.'

'Let's hope Jonathan never finds out about them,' she said. 'Not that I'd sign one.'

While we contemplated that scenario, the door flew open, startling us both.

'Are you want me clean bedroom attic?' asked a forty-something woman with deep-red hair and fantastic bone structure. A hand slowly rose and covered her nose.

'Yes. Please. Milena,' said Astrid, either enunciating clearly or trying not to sound wasted. She wafted fingers under her nose. 'Sorry, Milena. Incense!'

Milena went off without shutting the door, laughing her way across the garden.

'Oh, shit,' said Astrid.

Back in the house, we had tea. It was from Fortnum & Mason and very nice. We then sat at Astrid's sparkling white table on two modern but comfy bucket dining chairs. I'd never noticed them, not before décor had become a scary looming issue for me. We talked about the boys – her son, Jakob, and my grandson, Alfie – and about what series and films we'd been watching.

'Right!' Astrid suddenly stood up, picked up a dinky yellow leather rucksack and wove her arms through it. 'Come on, then,' she said, gesturing towards the front door.

'Er, where?' I asked, slowly rising.

She opened a drawer and took out a tape measure. 'If I'm going to design your kitchen, I'll need to see it first.'

'Oh, Astrid!' I stepped towards her with open arms, but up went the palm of her hand with its don't-you-dare rays.

* * *

We walked to my house, where Gary and Astrid hit it off immediately, both being practical, straight-talking, and right up there on the frightening scale. I left them in the kitchen, one either end of Astrid's tape measure, and went upstairs to root out at least one other semi-glam outfit, just in case Billy decided not to do a runner. I went for black this time, a dress that had seen me through a decade of nights out and funerals. It was a bit dusty and for some reason smelled of glue – or just an aroma of building site – but I shoved it in a bag, along with beads for colour and another pair of shoes.

It was ten to twelve. I needed to get back to the hotel and do a bit of Jessica research on my laptop before the two o'clock meeting in the office. How I'd concentrate on Jessica when my head was filled with Billy I didn't know. We'd talked and talked until late, had sex, ordered another bottle and drunk most of it, then slept a bit, then gone for a long walk around two in the morning, then slept until past nine, when he'd woken, looked at his phone, sworn, dressed hurriedly, kissed me with a 'See you later,' and shot out the door.

It was odd that I wasn't tired, what with having had barely any sleep, but that's what love does, I guessed, as I got in my car and thought to hell with the hotel parking fees. I'd sign up for more supply teaching.

* * *

'So, what have we got?' snapped Mike, seconds after I walked through the door with an apology for being late. It was about ten past two, so I wasn't sure I deserved the sour face. 'Edie, do you want to start?'

He was sitting in my chair, behind my desk. I took the one next to Emily and was forced to look up at Mike in his elevated position. Be magnanimous, I told myself. Mike was a partner in Fox Wilder, after all. Or rather, he would be once he'd sold his house and put in the loosely agreed sum.

'OK,' I said, placing my laptop on the desk and opening it. 'Jessica seems to be running a successful catering business, which has gradually moved into full-scale events management. There are around ten franchises–'

'Eighteen,' said Mike. 'According to Em.'

'Right.' I peered at the Jessica Relish website, floundering and feeling my cheeks warm. I turned to Emily. 'Want to take over with what you know, Em?'

I caught Mike pursing his lips, then Emily read from her phone, reeling off dates, figures, and even gross and net profits. 'Their USP is that they strive to source locally grown food whenever possible, prioritising organic products and meat from farmers with certified animal-welfare standards.'

I nodded to show I too had discovered these things. I hadn't. In fact, after a cursory glance at Jessica's website, I'd had a sudden energy crash and taken a much-needed nap. Hence my late arrival.

'Also,' said Emily, looking up from her script, 'they say they're ninety-five per cent single-use-plastic free?'

'Yes, I saw that,' said Mike.

'Anything on Hugh?' I asked, cleverly changing the subject.

Mike leaned back in my chair and swivelled, fingers linked on his tummy. He waited a while before speaking. 'Not on Facebook. Doesn't do Twitter or Instagram. Or he stopped, knowing his wife was monitoring him.'

'Anything else?'

'Well, yesterday evening, Em and I decided we'd get Jessica out of the flat this morning by asking her to bring some ID into the office. Emily reminded her that we were obliged to check. While she was out, I had a quick look around her place. It's a ground-floor flat, with a garden. Very nice.'

'I'm sorry?' I asked. 'You did what?'

'I only intended to see if there was a smashed-up bike in the back garden, which there wasn't. Only then, well, I tried the back door and it wasn't locked, so... I know, I know, but the temptation was too great. It's a gorgeous flat. Oh, yeah, and I took photos.' He grimaced and showed them to me.

'Honestly, Mike,' I said, enjoying him now being in the doghouse. Yes, it did look rather lovely. I passed his phone to Emily, who said, 'Cool,' to each shot.

'I'm sorry for not including you, Edie. Only when I left you at the hotel yesterday evening, you seemed a bit... let's just say tired.'

I was colouring up again, damn. Could it be the menopause? 'Yes, I was.'

'Did you notice the neighbours' houses?' Emily asked. 'I mean, did it look like they've got students in, or what? I know some people in Divinity Road, like, halfway up, before it gets posh at the top.'

'Yeah, the houses either side did look a bit, you know, shared. Studenty. But then they seemed to improve further along. As you say, the higher, the posher. Oh, hang on, I took a couple of outside photos.' He got them up and showed us a row of four or five houses and a close-up of Jessica and Hugh's flat.

'Aha!' said Emily. 'Can you forward those to me, Mike?'

'Sure,' he said. 'I'll send them all.' From the look on his face, he was as baffled as I was.

'And me?' I asked.

'Yep... there you go... Emily... Edie... done.'

'Thanks,' I said. 'I think I'd like to talk to Jessica again. Buy her a drink and get her to open up a bit more, and maybe come up with some places where Hugh could be that she hadn't thought of. People she hadn't thought of. We'll obviously look into Zara, but she could be as clueless as Jessica, if he's left her too.'

'Unless she's hiding him,' said Mike. 'Protecting Hugh from his wife, as Jessica suggested.'

Emily raised her arm.

'You don't need to do that, Em,' Mike said.

'Shit, keep forgetting.' She lowered it again. 'I was wondering if we should, like, watch the flat? Jessica's flat? It could be that when she goes back to London, Hugh might turn up there? Or him and Zara? Or even when Jessica goes out?"

Mike and I looked at each other.

'Might be worth it,' I said, 'but how? We can only sit in cars for so long, plus it's mostly residents' parking there.'

'I know,' said Emily, 'but I might have a way of doing it. Let me check it out first, yeah?'

'OK, but you will be discreet?'

'I will.' She put her phone in her shirt pocket and stood up. 'Is it OK if I…?' She nodded at the door. 'Before my shift, I've got an assignment to do on the ethics of private investigation. You know, Mike, like not breaking and entering?' She laughed and hooked her cloth bag over one shoulder.

'I'll have you know,' said Mike, 'I didn't break a thing.'

* * *

Mike and I went for a late lunch at Cat Burger, where we got my favourite window table, and I astonished Mike by ordering Cat's vegan burger.

'I'm on a health kick,' I explained.

'Since when?'

'It's been gradual.'

I could have said since Billy told me he was veggie and that he'd find it hard to be in a relationship with a meat eater.

Mike was sniggering. 'I can get you discounted gym membership, if you want?'

'Er, yeah.' I'd never used a gym, not since leaving school. 'Thanks.'

When our meals arrived, Mike lifted my chunky chips and said, 'Tut tut, Edie,' then swapped them for his sweet potato fries. I wondered how something fried and with sweet in its name could be healthy, but they tasted great.

We agreed we'd try and get Jessica out for lunch or dinner the next day. After a few drinks, perhaps she'd open up a bit more about Hugh's contacts, male and female. She'd told us she'd be heading back to London at the weekend, and I still needed to catch up on sleep, so there was only a small window.

I tried her phone while still with Mike, and she said she could only do a quick coffee at half ten the next day.

'Shall we meet in the café by the office?' I asked.

'Um. Yes, OK. I er… Oh, never mind. I'll see you in there.'

'Odd,' I told Mike after the call. 'It was like she wanted to tell me something.'

'Perhaps she will tomorrow?'

'Hope so.'

Mike and I parted on the Cowley Road, and I looked again to see if Billy had been in touch. He hadn't.

* * *

Back at the hotel there was still no word from Billy – real name Ben, it turned out. I'd told him about Emily's Ben, our friendly and useful policeman, and asked if I could call him Billy. After googling Billy Bob Thornton, he'd agreed to it on the condition he could call me Angelina. 'I think that might jinx us,' I'd said, presuming there would be an 'us'. Right now, I was beginning to doubt it.

I decided to take it easy for the rest of the day and start work on the case tomorrow, once I'd caught up on sleep and my brain was unfogged. I took a long bath with a large glass of room-delivered Chablis to help me relax and an Eckhart Tolle book to help me live in the now. I dropped off for a while, then woke to see it was almost five, and there was still nothing from Billy. OK, he was at work busily framing pictures, but he could have found time to send a message. I'd have been happy with "Hey, sorry I had to dash off this morning." Billy ran his own business too, so I should really have understood.

When we'd met, he'd been delivering a picture to an elderly client from Cheltenham. She'd never have navigated her way to his premises, tucked away behind the Pegasus Youth Theatre, so he'd suggested meeting at the hotel. He employed two other framers and a 'godsend' of an admin woman called Georgia, whose name he'd said so often that I'd pretty much hated her by midnight.

Reminding myself that women and men communicate differently, and that men tend to compartmentalise, I returned to Eckhart and learned about first acknowledging, then letting go of unwanted thoughts. Live in the moment, then live in the next moment was the advice.

I gave it a go. *I'm in the bath, relaxed on wine, concentrating on my breathing...*

He'd have to go home after work, of course, all the way to a village five miles from Oxford. Then he'd have to feed Noah, his useless-sounding son. 'He'd live on peanut-butter sandwiches,' Billy had said, 'if it wasn't for me.'

Noah was twenty-six, only slightly younger than Maeve. Maeve fed half of Brighton, but Noah couldn't cook for himself?

'It's very tiring,' Billy had said in his son's defence, 'working on the tills in the Co-op.'

Perhaps Billy's phone had run out of charge and he'd left his charger at home?

I'm in the bath, relaxed on wine, concentrating on my breathing...

He could be a player, of course. Or he'd realised he didn't fancy me after all.

I'm in the bath, relaxed on—

My phone rang. I picked it up and saw an unfamiliar number. Was it his? I hadn't saved him as a contact, fearing it would be tempting fate.

'Hello?' I said, as husky as I could manage.

'Am I speaking to Edie Fox?' asked a rather flat male voice.

I cleared my throat. 'Yes, that's me.'

'My name's Detective Sergeant Andy Laing of Thames Valley Police, Cowley.'

'Oh, right.' I sat up and hoped he wouldn't hear water sloshing.

'I'm sorry to disturb you, Ms Fox, but I was wondering if you'd be able to come into the station?'

My heart started racing. This was a 'now' I didn't want to be living in. 'You mean today?'

'If you wouldn't mind.'

'Can I ask why?'

'Yes. We're investigating a missing person and believe you may be able to help with our inquiries. I tried your office, then called at your home address. Your builder said you were staying in a hotel but didn't know which one. Would you mind telling us? We could always send a car for you, if that's more convenient.'

Now my heart was galloping. Had I unknowingly knocked someone into the canal at two in the morning on my drunken walk with Billy? Been caught on camera? I cursed Gary for not calling or texting me to say the police had dropped by. Given me a heads up.

'No need to send a car, I can walk to you in ten minutes.'

'Thank you, Miss Fox. Just ask for me, DS Laing, at the desk.'

'I will,' I said, now feeling sick.

He thanked me again and we hung up. Why couldn't I have asked who was missing? I was thrown by the call, of course. But by not asking, had I made myself some kind of suspect?

I hauled myself out of the bath, dressed, and rubbed my damp hair with a towel. I found a flapjack in the bottom of my bag, ate it to soak up the wine, brushed my teeth and swigged at mouthwash, shuddering at its alcoholic sting. It gave me a headache, or perhaps that was the wine. I was never going to drink again. At least, not alone.

The weather had finally taken a turn for the cooler, and it felt around a perfect eighteen or nineteen degrees. It had rained, I noticed, at some point. Roll on proper autumn, I thought as I walked. I couldn't wait to be wearing jumpers and boots and kicking at piles of crispy red leaves. Also, the warm light and long shadows of autumn saw Oxford's stone colleges at their best. I'd upgrade my phone to one like Emily's and take stunning photos to amaze my would-be Instagram followers.

These musings were a distraction, of course, and when the police station reared into view, I felt my insides fill with the terror as I began rolling through people I knew who might be missing. It couldn't be Billy. Or could it? Perhaps there was a wife after all, worried that he'd stayed out all night for the first time in thirty years.

* * *

'Hugh Horsfield,' said DS Laing.

We weren't in an interrogation room, as I'd pictured, but at a corner desk in a bustling open-plan office. There was no two-way mirror or machine to record me, just Detective Sergeant Andy Laing holding up a photo of Jessica's husband. Andy Laing was early thirties, at a guess, and sounded very south London. It brought back memories of my grandparents on my mother's side.

'I've never met him,' I said. 'Only his wife, Jessica. She came into the office yesterday, asking us to find Hugh.'

'You run a private investigation agency, is that right?'

'Well…' I was flushing again for some reason. Because I was with an actual proper detective? I shrugged. 'Yes, but it's very much a part-time thing. My father was a policeman and I was tempted to become one too, but you know, life and teaching got in the way.'

DS Laing attempted a smile. After putting down Hugh's photo, he picked up his pen. 'Could you tell me what happened when Jessica came to see you? What she said?'

'OK.' I wondered how much I should tell him. What was confidential, if anything? I summarised Jessica's visit, then asked, 'Who reported Hugh missing?'

'Zara Peacock. The girlfriend.'

'Ah.'

'Do you know her?'

'Yes. I mean no. It was the name Jessica gave us. She couldn't find Hugh to serve him divorce papers, but knew he'd been seeing Zara. Jessica hadn't wanted to contact Zara herself. How long has Hugh been missing?'

'Just over two weeks, according to Zara.'

'Do you think something's happened to him?'

DS Laing closed his notebook and blinked, slowly. 'I doubt it. People disappear for all sorts of reasons. Let's say we're not ruling anything out, or anything in...' He blinked again but this time his eyes remained closed. Then they sprang open. 'Right!' he said with a small jerk. 'Would you mind if we took a statement from you? I'll get one of my DCs to come over and–'

'I'm so sorry,' I said, pulling my phone from a pocket. A written, signed statement? I wasn't sure I should, not without consulting my contract with Jessica. 'I have a meeting in, oh crikey, five minutes ago.' I picked up my bag and stood. 'Could I do it another time?'

He went to answer but couldn't suppress an enormous yawn. He covered it with a hand and shook his head awake. 'Excuse me. New baby. Come in as soon as poss, yeah?'

'I will,' I said. 'And congratulations.'

'Thanks, but commiserations might be more apt. We've got three under five now. I haven't slept for four and a half years.'

'It'll get better,' I reassured him. But what did I know? I'd had just the one baby who'd slept like, well, a baby. She still did.

He looked doubtful. He also looked dazed and completely knackered. If I accidentally forgot to come in and make a statement, would he even notice?

* * *

As soon as I was a decent distance from the station, I called Mike to update him on Hugh.

'Jesus,' he said. 'How did this DS Laing know about our connection with Jessica? Did she tell him?'

'I didn't ask, but I'm sure that's why she was a bit odd on the phone. Anyway, all I could think about was getting out of there before I breached my contract with her.'

'Understandable. Although it's not like you're her lawyer or doctor.'

'I know.'

'I guess now our search should focus on Hugh.'

'I don't know,' I said. 'What if Zara is still in on it? She and Hugh could be getting Jessica worked up to the point of agreeing to a fifty-fifty divorce split.'

'Maybe.'

'I think I'll keep my appointment with Jessica tomorrow morning, if she still wants to meet. If she still has faith in us. I'd like to see how she is now and what she wants us to do. Emily could come too.'

'OK. And while you're there, I might try out brunch at Nice Buns.'

'In disguise?'

'Of course.'

I had a quick think. 'Listen, why don't we all meet first thing tomorrow at the office? Have a chinwag.'

He laughed. 'Yes, let's have a chinwag.'

'Nine fifteen?'

'Yep.'

'OK. I'll tell Emily.'

'Great. Oh, and Edie?'

'What?'

'Try not to be late, yeah? Remember you have to meet Jessica at ten thirty.'

I wasn't sure when exactly thirty-four-year-old Mike had turned into my parent, but I let it go.

I called Emily and told her what had happened.

'Oh no!' she said. 'Poor Jessica's never going to get her divorce if even Zara's lost him. Shall I ask Ben to find out what they know?'

'That would be really useful.' I repeated what I'd told Mike about wanting to get out of the station before I breached client confidentiality.

'You mean cos if you lie or omit things in a statement, you'd be, like, perverting the course of justice and could go away for six months?'

'Shit, is that true?' Since starting her online diploma in private investigation, Emily had become our go-to legal expert.

'Just done a module on it. Six months is the maximum, so you might get less, say two. I could ask Ben–'

'No! Just stick to the Hugh stuff. Please.'

'I wouldn't mention you, honest. I'm always asking him things that help with my coursework.'

'Even so, I'd rather you didn't. See you in the office at nine fifteen?'

'Yeah, OK.'

A number I didn't recognise was trying to call me. DS Laing again?

'Got to go,' I told Emily and answered the incoming call with a very polite, 'Hello?'

'Edie?' asked Billy.

I felt my heart lift. 'This is she.'

'Sorry, didn't sound like you.'

'It's been a bit of a day.'

'Yeah, for me too. Jeez, my head hurts. I was so tired, I spent two hours putting the wrong frame on a client's portrait of her ugly husband, and now I'll have to look at him again tomorrow.'

'I'm sorry.'

'I should think so too. Want to repeat it?'

'Tonight?' I asked.

'Very funny. I'll need a couple of days to recover. And I've got something on Saturday, but how about Sunday evening? Are you free?'

I paused, not knowing what to do.

'Edie?' said Billy. 'Sorry, is that too long to be away from me?'

'Ha ha. No, I'm actually going to a gig on Sunday. My assistant's boyfriend is playing in a pub on Cowley Road. The Oxford Scholar.' I crossed my fingers and asked if he wanted to come.

'Er… I don't know. Did you say he's a copper?'

'He is. Well remembered!'

'Thanks, miss.'

'Oops, sorry. Just comes naturally.'

He chuckled endearingly. 'I actually like it. The teacher thing.'

'Pervert.'

'Can't deny it.'

I laughed. I also hoped he wasn't actually a pervert. That I wouldn't have to dress up as Nanny, or Matron, or Mrs Thatcher. Then I remembered he'd been to state schools and relaxed and let out a long sigh.

'Are you bored?' Billy asked.

'Sorry, miles away. Listen, do come on Sunday. There'll be other oldies there.'

'Truthfully?'

'Cross my heart. The students aren't back yet.'

'OK then.'

We agreed that he'd come to the hotel at seven. The Off Beats were due to play at nine, so that would give us time to have a bite to eat and a drink before the rush, if there was a rush. With the lack of students, the band would have to rely on locals turning up. In an effort to rally support, I'd even mentioned it to Gary and his guys.

'I had a lovely time,' said Billy.

'Me too.'

'You're just saying that because I did.'

'No, no. I enjoyed our… a lot.'

'Good. You said you'd had quite a day? Want to talk about it?'

'Not right now, but thanks. Maybe on Sunday?'

We both said we were looking forward to it, then Billy's son came home and called something out to his dad.

'He's reaching for the peanut butter,' said Billy. 'Better go.'

I stared at my phone for a while, my heart in a knot. What exactly was he doing on Saturday? And who with? That was the problem with having experience of cheating, lying, scumbag partners like Bloody Greg; the insecurity, or paranoia, never quite leaves you.

Billy had mentioned his mother being in a home. Perhaps he always visited her on Saturdays? I managed to convince myself, as I walked back to the hotel, that Billy would be driving home from visiting his mother in her distant care home on Saturday evening, whilst very much looking forward to our date.

Back in my room, after a calming cup of tea, I sat cross-legged on the bed with a pen and A4 pad. The aim was to write a list of things for the team to investigate or research and any questions I might have for Jessica. But after an hour or so, I woke up from one of those chin-on-chest naps, and saw I'd got no further than "Jessic".

FIVE

The alarm had gone off at seven, giving me enough time to fit in a veggie fry-up in the hotel restaurant before driving to my house and quickly checking that Gary hadn't been browbeaten by Astrid.

'Charming and attractive woman,' he said, continuing to saw at a length of skirting board, then stopping to wipe his brow. He tapped the side of his head. 'Got a lot going on up here as well.'

'She has,' I agreed.

'Wanted to know if she should consult you before purchasing anything. I told her not to bother, and she said, "Oh good cause it's not exactly Edie's forte", then she told me some stories and we had a right laugh.'

Stories about me? I wasn't sure how I felt about not being consulted, but then I imagined getting into a disagreement with Astrid over splashbacks or whatever, and her storming off without finishing the job, and me losing a good friend. Well, a friend. Kind of.

I apologised to Gary for the police calling in, and wrote down on the back an envelope which hotel I was staying at and handed it to him. 'Just in case anyone else is after me.'

He tucked it into his shirt pocket, then shook his head while his eyes roamed over the new extension. 'Let's pray it's not anyone about building regs,' he said. I thought he might wink and say, 'Just kidding,' but he didn't.

* * *

I was in the office before the others, so I reclaimed my desk and chair and pulled up the notes I'd written on my laptop. The previous evening, after the early doze, my brain had suddenly found the ability to function. I'd worked for two hours or so, moving back and forth between the bed and the small table, sustaining myself with the room's free biscuits and hot chocolate. Afterwards, I'd watched a bit of news, then got under the duvet around eleven and fallen into a deep sleep. A whole evening without alcohol. I'd done well. Obviously, the Chablis in the bath didn't count. That had been in the afternoon.

I began to read through my notes, ready for my coffee with Jessica.

'Hey, Edie,' said Emily a few minutes later. It was only nine, but she was always either punctual or early.

'Hi, Em. How are you?'

'I'm good. Can I make you a cuppa?'

'I'm all right, thanks. But perhaps a jug of iced water for all of us?'

'Coming up.' She took a bunch of mint, a cucumber, a lemon and two limes from her bag and returned three minutes later with a clinking jug and three glasses on a tray.

'Is that tray new?' I asked.

'Yeah, saw it in a charity shop and thought it might be useful?'

'It's nice. You do know you can claim back any expenses, right?'

'Nah, no need. I mean, you're paying for my course.'

'So I am. How's that going?' It felt like ages since I'd caught up with her.

'Really well. Got good marks for my assignments, so far.'

'Uh-huh.' Notifications for two emails popped up on my laptop.

'I'm, like, averaging As?'

'Wow, that's fantastic. Keep it up, won't you?'

'I'll try.'

One email was from Astrid. That would keep. The other was from Jessica. I opened it quickly. It was brief, so I read it out loud. 'Please could we cancel coffee later. Am on my way to your office now. Hope that's OK, Jessica.'

'Oh, shit,' said Emily. 'Why didn't she text like a normal person?' She jumped up and grabbed her phone. 'We need to warn Mike not to come in. I'll go down to the shop and make sure they don't meet.'

'I'm calling him now,' I said. Mike picked up. 'Where are you?' I asked.

'Next door, getting a coffee. Want anything?'

'No, thanks, but listen, Jessica's on her way here. We just heard.'

'Damn.'

'Em's gone down to meet her. I'll alert you when she leaves.'

'Yeah, do that.'

A few minutes later, Jessica walked into the office wearing a long-sleeved baggy top and faded skinny jeans. Her hair was tied back in a scrunchy, and she wore no make-up. I'd have walked past her in the street.

'Hi Jessica,' I said. 'Have a seat.'

'Thanks.'

'Would you like some water?' asked Emily, following her in.

'Please.'

Emily poured water and chunks of adornments into a glass and handed it to Jessica, then filled two more.

'Did the police talk to you?' asked Jessica.

'They did,' I said. 'Someone called DS Laing.'

'Yes, sorry. Thought I'd better tell them I'd seen you.' She picked a chunk of cucumber out of her glass and looked around for somewhere to put it.

'Here,' said Emily, cupping her hands.

'It disagrees with me,' Jessica explained, dropping the cucumber, then tapping her tummy. 'Sorry, Emily.'

'No, I'm sorry. Should've asked. I'm like that with radishes. Like, one radish and I'm on the Rennies for days.'

'Hah, don't get me started on radishes!' They both laughed, then Jessica turned her mascara-free eyes back to me. 'So,' she said, 'Hugh really has done a runner.'

'The police didn't tell me any details, only that he's been missing for a couple of weeks and that it was Zara who reported it.'

Jessica nodded. 'My guess is Zara went to the police because he'd been relying on her for financial support after I'd stopped providing it.'

'And she wondered how he could be surviving without it?'

'Either that, or he's left her, owing her thousands, and she wants to root him out to claw some of it back.'

'I like that theory,' said Emily.

'Me too,' said Jessica. 'You always want your ex to dump his new love. Serves her right! She wasn't that great after all!'

'That's so true,' I said. 'Do you mind if I ask when and why Hugh left you? We didn't really get that far in the café, did we?'

'No, sorry. I expect I was rambling.'

'Not at all, but if you could fill us in on the time between the accident in the early summer and his leaving?'

'Of course. OK, so… let me think. Well, things weren't great after my accident. I was on strong painkillers and had several courses of antibiotics to try and shift the infection I'd picked up in hospital. My arm was still in a sling.'

'Poor you,' said Emily.

'Yeah, it was a bit rough. We'd had to cancel our holiday in France because I wasn't feeling up to it. My inner control freak didn't think Hugh and the boys could manage it on their own.' She grimaced. 'Not that inner, perhaps. There was huge disappointment, but Derek and good-egg Pippa stepped in and took the boys off to Greece for a fortnight. That was, what? The end of July? The summer is a bit of a blur, thanks to the codeine.'

'So, you and Hugh were left alone?' I said before Emily could tell codeine tales.

Jessica sighed. 'Yes.'

'And how was that?'

'Ghastly, to be honest, what with Hugh finally discovering I'd been tracking his phone and completely losing it. Calling me the C-word over and over. Despite his bad behaviour, he'd never, ever spoken to me that way. It was so upsetting, and I remember crying a lot and wondering where old Hugh had gone. It all got too much for me, making work impossible. So, towards the end of that first week, while the boys were in Greece and Hugh was extremely cross with me, I felt I needed a break and took myself off to a friend's empty cottage in Dorset.

Ross, my PA, drove me there. When I got back five days later, Hugh had gone.'

'You mean gone gone?' asked Emily.

'Totally.' Jessica inhaled shakily. 'He'd taken everything of his and several things of mine, including my great-grandmother's engagement ring and other jewellery items, plus designer dresses, handbags and shoes.' She got out her phone and showed us some photos. 'These three paintings by young artists disappeared too. They could already be worth a small fortune.'

'That's terrible,' I said. 'Did you report the theft?'

'I didn't. You know, the boys…' She looked up and smiled. 'I have this vision of her – Zara – in her little caff, wearing my Stella McCartney to dish up Scotch egg with packet salad.'

'Do you think he guessed you'd cut off his money?' asked Emily. 'That's why he took the stuff?'

'Undoubtedly.' She put her glass of water down, picked up her bag, and pointed in the direction of the café next door. 'I'd love a decent coffee. Shall we…? Unless you have other clients to see?'

'Let me just…' I pretended to check my phone's calendar but was texting Mike to leave. 'Um, no. Not for a while.'

SIX

'As I told you,' said Jessica once we'd settled at a table, 'I don't remember the accident itself – actually coming off the bike. Only the feeling of being out of control as I whizzed down Divinity Road. Trying the brakes over and over again and panicking.'

'Do you know who called for an ambulance?' I asked.

'No, I don't. A passer-by, I suppose. Hugh said he made some enquiries, but since no other vehicle appeared to have been involved, there was no police report. They think I must have crashed into a bollard. No witnesses close enough to see exactly what happened.'

Emily arrived with a flat white for Jessica, a tea for me and a cold drink for herself. I'd never seen her drink anything warm. All part of the lengthened childhood they have now. At least Maeve had had a child and moved on to hot liquids. My own mother had put tea in my baby bottle. I told Emily what Jessica had just said and she tapped it in her phone.

'I do wonder,' said Jessica, 'if Zara's simply protecting him from me until he can get a better divorce settlement. Something like that?'

'We were wondering the same,' I said.

Emily nodded. 'And like going to the police, who will most likely do fuck all to find him, 'scuse my French, is like a cover?'

'Quite. And I'm sure that to the police he's just a Jack the Lad who's left first one woman, then another.'

'On the other hand,' said Emily, 'it's hard to imagine Zara taking the risk? Like, wasting police time is an offence.'

Jessica stared into her cup. 'I don't know her, so have no idea if she'd take that risk. Love makes you do daft things.'

'Tell me about it,' said Emily.

I scanned my list of questions. 'Would Hugh have any other reason to disappear? No dodgy people after him, or some other woman's husband?'

'Like Zara's?' she asked.

'Does she have a husband?'

'I believe, Edie,' said Jessica, leaning in and taking a slice of cake, 'that's for you to find out.'

She winked, and I decided I quite liked her.

We paid up and left. 'What next?' Jessica asked, when out in the street. 'As I said, I'm happy to get in touch with Hugh's parents. Get them to check their weekend place in Norfolk.'

'OK. And Emily and I will discuss everything you've told us and take it from there.'

'It's just the two of you, is it?'

'Yeah, that's right,' said Emily.

'So, you're Emily Wilder, are you? As in Fox Wilder?'

'I wish,' she said.

Oh, Emily.

I sensed the wheels and cogs kicking in as she wound a pretty scarf that matched her pink hair around her. She'd recently had a small tattoo removed from her neck – someone's name – so she often wore scarves.

'We've got this sleeping partner,' she said. 'Mr Wilder. Arthur. He doesn't like attention, so we don't mention him on the website.'

'I see.'

'But we often hire others on a freelance basis,' I added, in case we came across as too small and too female, with only one elderly patron. 'And Arthur isn't our only investor.'

There was also me. In fact, only me.

Jessica gave a satisfied nod. 'Keep me posted,' she said as she slowly backed off. 'I've decided to hang around here for a bit longer. The boys won't give a toss. They love having my mum there. Deliveroo every day and no fresh fruit. And who knows, maybe Hugh will roll up at the flat here, tail between his legs.'

'Here's hoping,' I said.

Emily and I walked through the shop, saying 'Hi,' to her brother and getting the usual grumpy response. If ever there was a person unhappy in his work, it was Oscar.

'I saw you were still in the café,' Mike said, once we were upstairs. 'Thought I could hide if you all came back.'

He was behind my desk again but this time he stood up and let me have it. 'How was it?'

'Interesting.'

Emily agreed. 'What about you, Arthur?'

She and I laughed.

'What's the joke?' he asked. 'Em?'

'That's your name if ever you meet Jessica? Sorry, it just like popped into my head.'

Mike unfolded his arms and grinned. 'I like it. Very Peaky Blinders.'

'Oh, and you're a sleeping partner,' I chipped in.

'Ha! Hardly sleeping.' He told us he'd been to Nice Buns and discovered Zara's brother Jamie there, serving. 'Someone asked after Zara, and he said she was staying at her parents' house.'

'Maybe she and Hugh are hiding out there?' said Emily.

'Maybe,' I said. 'Actually, I've been doing a bit of research on her and her family.' I thought I caught a brief doubtful glance between Mike and Emily. 'What I've found out so far,' I continued, 'is that Zara Peacock is twenty-nine, and after dropping out of an international relations degree, became a traveller. India, Thailand, and so on. All on Facebook. I sent her a friend request last night under a made-up name with a blurry photo of Maeve, and she accepted it straight away. That's the good thing about travellers, they think they must have met you somewhere in the world.'

I looked up and saw that the doubt in Emily and Mike's expressions had eased.

'Anyway,' I continued, 'she returned to Oxfordshire two years ago, bought the lease on an ailing café in Headington, and turned it around. Her surname is unusual, and as far as my searches went, I couldn't find a husband. She didn't say her relationship status on Facebook, and photos didn't show her with one particular partner. Assuming her parents were also Peacock, I found their address in a village the other side of Witney. They run a storage and removals company from the premises next to their house.'

I pulled up two photos on my laptop and showed them the first. 'Nice, eh?' It was a beautiful old Cotswold stone house that had been sensitively extended on either side. 'And then this is the business... the storage block is all self-service units. Money for old rope, if you ask me. And here's the fleet of vans. Dad, Jerry, belongs to the local Rotary Club and Mum, Fiona, who's also busy on Facebook but doesn't know or care about privacy settings, does the books for the business. The couple holiday abroad a lot, but also seem to have a place on the south coast they retreat to in the UK. Couldn't work out exactly where that was, though. Zara's brother, Jamie, did a criminology degree at Cardiff University and graduated in June. I'm not sure why he'd be working in his sister's café, but he could just be helping out during a difficult time.'

'Wow,' said Emily.

'Ditto,' said Mike.

'I got carried away,' I told them, 'but luckily, eh? Since Zara's now staying at her parents' house.'

'You must've been a bit psychic,' said Emily. 'I get that a lot.'

'This we've noticed,' said Mike. 'Still no luck with the lottery, though?'

'Uh-uh. It's just so random, my psychic thing. Like the other day, I was cycling here to do a shift in the shop, and in my head I saw an old man in a colourful beanie buying a melon. One of the yellow ones? And there he was when I walked in. At the till, paying for a yellow watermelon and wearing a, like, rainbow beanie. I mean, they're never earth-shattering premonitions...'

Mike grinned at her. 'But should lottery numbers ever pop into your head...'

'Yeah, yeah,' she said, laughing. 'Listen. I reckon we should still keep an eye on Jessica's flat. Like I said, see if anyone goes there when she eventually heads back to

London. Hugh, or Zara, or whoever. And… thing is, I've like got this friend, sort of, called Toby, who lives opposite Jessica on Divinity Road. First-floor flat. He's got a great view of her front door. I went there yesterday.'

'Oh?' I said. 'Don't suppose he works from home and would like to make extra cash doing surveillance?'

'He does work from home, only it's not exactly work, and it's not exactly legal, if you get my drift?'

'Oh, Christ. No, Em, we can't employ a drug-dealer friend. Sorry.'

'Actually, Toby's not a friend. I hate him, even though I've like tried so hard over and over to forgive him for what he did to me, or let me do to myself. Got to take some responsibility, haven't I?'

'Well… you were young and lost.'

'Yeah, just Toby's type. So, yesterday, right? That was the first time I've been back to that disgusting place for years. Made me sick, but I had this idea. I thought maybe we could use him by, like, helping him?'

'Want to explain?' asked Mike.

'Well, I accidentally, only not really, broke a pane of glass. Secretly cut the sash cord and let the window drop, then I gave it a bit of a hard tap and cracked it.' She must have seen our faces. 'No, no, don't worry, he didn't see.'

'That's not really the point, Em,' said Mike, as if he had a leg to stand on.

'I know, sorry. But I thought if I paid someone to fix it, they could watch Jessica's flat. Someone trustworthy who won't snitch on Toby. I actually told him I worked with someone exactly like that.'

I looked at Mike, and so did Emily.

'No, no,' he said, pretending to be pissed off.

'Toby like gave me a set of keys. Said he sleeps all day, so…'

'OK, Em,' said Mike. 'I'll find out how to do it on YouTube.'

'Brilliant! I couldn't sleep last night trying to think of someone.'

'Thanks, Mike,' I said. 'No getting hooked on anything, though.'

'Nah, not me. Drugs have never been my thing, unless you count multivitamins. The gym, though, that's another story.'

'Ben's hooked on the gym as well,' sighed Emily. 'Luckily for me. I tell you, he can go on for–'

'La, la, la.' I stuck my fingers in my ears. I'd have to have that word with her.

Mike, oblivious, rubbed his bristly chin. 'I'm thinking the window job might take up to three or four days, if I insist on painting the frame. Of course, I could pack it in before that if there's nothing to see at Jessica's or something more urgent comes along.'

We wound up the meeting and agreed we'd catch up with one another on Sunday at the gig. Mike was going to research sash window repairs, and Emily would sound out Ben about how the police investigation was going – or if there even was one. I was going to take a trip out to the village of Fellford to see the Peacocks' place and maybe have a nose around, pretend I needed to store some things.

Mike left first, then Emily and I stood out on the pavement chatting.

'Are you OK?' I asked. 'After seeing Toby yesterday?' I knew there'd been a bad-news boyfriend in her past.

'I'm fine, thanks. Except...'

'What?'

'There was this girl there, in his flat. Daisy? Maybe seventeen or even sixteen, hard to tell. She reminded me of me, back then, before I got clean. She just sort of sat there staring at nothing, not even a phone. Then she'd sometimes like smile stupidly at Toby when he was laughing at something he'd said that he thought was hilarious. It's like that Stockholm thing?'

'Stockholm syndrome?'

'That's it. He wasn't always, you know, kind, either. More with his words, but he'd, like, lash out every now and then.'

'He hit you?'

She nodded.

'So he's a dealer who hits young women. You have to report him, Em.'

'I know. But if he got arrested, what would happen to Daisy? It's so hard when you're addicted and got no money and you can't go home.'

'Rehab?'

'That's impossible to get into unless you can pay.'

'Sorry,' I said. 'I'm not being much help.'

'Yeah, you are. Cos you listen.'

'Any time,' I told her. 'Don't do anything rash without talking to me, though.' We had a good hug then walked to the corner of my street. 'See you Sunday evening.'

'Yeah, cool. You know, I'm actually quite nervous about the gig.'

'Me too.' My first date with Billy.

'Oh, don't worry about being old, Edie.'

'Uh, thanks. I won't.'

'Even my dad might come along. Mum says he used to be a secret headbanger.'

I remembered Emily's parents from when she and Maeve were at school together. The girls were close, until Emily got moved to the other side of the city to a farmhouse that Steve and Linda lovingly and obsessively did up while their daughter secretly bunked off her crap new school.

'It'll be nice to see your parents again,' I said. 'In the meantime, let us know if you find out anything from Ben.'

'Will do.' She looked at her phone. 'Oops, late for my shift.'

She ran back into the shop, and I wondered what to do with myself. I decided to visit Gary. All was going well with the renovations, he said, although I could see no progress myself. While there, I remembered Astrid had emailed me, so got my phone out and opened the quote she'd attached.

'How much?' I cried in front of Gary.

'Give it here,' he said, and I handed the phone to him. I needed to sit down, but where?

Gary chortled. 'Shrewd businesswoman, that Astrid.'

I saw something in his expression. Love?

'To be fair,' he said, 'that does include a lot of the gubbins.'

I took another look and saw he was right; she had included materials, along with white goods. 'Even so…'

'What you wanna ask yourself, Edie, is what's the alternative?'

'An empty room with a concrete floor?'

'Quite.'

I replied to the email with a gushy yes and a gushy thank you. Astrid came back promptly with "Fab!" and a request for part-payment in advance for fixtures, fittings, paint, flooring, and miscellaneous decorative pieces. I wasn't sure I liked the sound of the last items, but since, out of ineptitude and laziness, I'd got myself well and truly over a barrel, I agreed to transfer several thousand pounds immediately.

"Thanks, Edie", she replied. "See you Sunday."

Of course, it was going to be worth the expense, I told myself while walking through the house to look at the lawn, which I imagined needed a good end-of-summer mow. But the lawn, I discovered, had more or less gone. My once pretty garden now grew planks of wood, concrete mixers, yet more plastic sheeting, and three young lads eating fish and chips.

Another job for Astrid, I immediately thought. Her garden was lovely and, of course, designed by her.

I gave the guys a wave and meandered my way back to the front door. 'Bye, Gary!' I called out. 'See you Sunday?'

He appeared in the hall, stroking his head. 'I dunno about—'

'Astrid's going,' I said, and left him with that.

SEVEN

When in Oxford, I usually video-called Alfie on Saturdays, then Maeve called me for a chat when she got a chance on Sundays. Having had a nice lie-in and a cuppa, I decided to skip the hotel's breakfast and speak to my much-missed grandson.

'Ha, ha, ha,' was the first thing he said, having been handed his mum's phone.

'What's funny?' I asked.

'Your hair!' he shouted, face filling my screen. 'Mummy, Mummy, Gran looks like Einstein!'

I tried flattening my hair, then Maeve appeared. 'Don't be sill— Oh, yeah, you do a bit. I think Gran's still in bed, Alfie.'

'Isn't he just five?' I asked, getting up and delving into my bag. I ran a comb through my bed hair. 'How does he know about Einstein?'

'YouTube, *Horrible Histories*. They know everything by five these days. Alfie, come back and talk to Gran. Tell her what you want to be when you grow up.' She whispered into the camera, 'It's so funny, the way he says quantum physicist.' She called him again. 'Remember what you told the man in the café when he asked what you wanted to be? Here, tell Gran.'

'A hair cutter!' Alfie shouted.

'No, no,' Maeve said. 'You know, the job that Milly's mum does?'

'If you're a hair cutter,' Alfie said, scarily close again, his huge brown eyes filling my screen, 'you can have a dragon drawed on your arm and a spider web on your neck, like George.'

'Did someone called George cut your hair?' I asked. I could see that it was quite a bit shorter. I often wished Maeve wouldn't lop off his beautiful dark curls.

'Yes!'

'And what job does Milly's mummy do?'

'She's a… Quan. Tum. Scissor. Sist,' he told me, nodding with each syllable.

'Wow,' I said, keeping a straight face, 'a quantum physicist. Wouldn't you like to be one of those?'

'No!'

'Why not?'

'Cos it's a girl's job!' Alfie did his loud fake ha-ha laugh again before disappearing.

Maeve was back on. 'Sorry, that's probably all you'll get out of him. He piled sugar on his pancakes when I wasn't looking.'

'Never mind. It's good to know you're bringing him up as a feminist.'

'I try,' she said. 'Although I suspect he thinks Quantum Scissorsists also cut hair. I'd better go, he's trying to ride Bear again. I'll get him to call you when he comes down.'

We ended the call, and I got back into bed. How lovely it was to have a couple of free hours to chill. I picked up *East of Eden* and began the first chapter.

What, I wondered, was I going to do once I'd laid eyes on the Peacock homestead? Play it by ear, I decided, rereading Steinbeck's first sentence of chapter one again. I'd grab a sandwich en route and eat it in the car.

I closed the book. What was I waiting for? I had a quick shower, blow-dried my Einstein, and looked up the route to Fellford.

Mike called as I was about to set off. He'd been back to Nice Buns and discovered Zara, Jamie and her parents were down at their place in Bournemouth.

'How did you… no, don't tell me.'

'Don't worry, I just used my ears.'

'Good. So… a good time to visit their house and business? Want to come?'

'I do. I can come get you in fifteen?'

I was about to protest – why do men always insist on driving – but he definitely had the more comfortable vehicle. 'Pick me up from my house? I need to swing by for a few things.'

'Okey-doke.'

* * *

'Do you do that thing I do?' I asked. 'That wherever you visit, you want to move there?'

We were driving through Fellford, a very pretty village on the Cotswold borders, with trees galore, the usual thatched and not-thatched houses, village green, two pubs and one shop with the Post Office sign outside.

'I could live here,' he said. 'For sure.'

'That's exactly what I'm thinking. Only I know I couldn't, not in reality.'

'Why not?' Mike checked the satnav. 'Around a mile to go.'

'I think I'd always feel there were rules, ones I didn't know or understand because I didn't grow up in the countryside. For example, what to plant in the front garden. I mean, does it have to be hollyhocks?'

'I believe it does.'

'And even once I got to know the rules, I'd feel a strong desire to rebel.'

'Grow pampas grass?'

'Exactly.'

We were coming out of the village now, with its 30 mph limit that no one was sticking to, not even when passing the speed camera Mike had slowed down for. They knew something we didn't. They must have some WhatsApp group that told them which cameras were disabled to save costs and where to buy the best hollyhock seeds.

'It should be coming up soon,' Mike said after we'd driven in silence for a bit. 'On the left.'

'Got it,' I said, following the route on my phone. 'Next turning.'

Mike pulled into a lay-by just past the entrance to the Peacocks' and switched off the engine.

'What's the plan, then?' he asked.

I unclipped my seatbelt and lifted a bag off the floor and onto my lap. 'I brought along one or two things. Not exactly to disguise myself, but perhaps stay covered in case of security cameras.'

While I delved in, Mike yanked his own much bigger bag from the back seat. 'For my undercover work,' he explained, then with the aid of the rear-view and sunshield mirrors, we both set to work, occasionally giving each other the thumbs up or thumbs down, or 'Christ, Mike, you look like a seventies assassin.'

We settled on a coordinated married-couple look. A married couple that the sun disagreed with. In the high-teens September temperature, we could just about get away with shades and sunhats. Mike had ditched the wig and sideburns that I'd found so disturbing and hid his shaved head under a Fedora. I'd pulled my hair into a ponytail that poked through the back of the baseball cap Greg had left behind.

'Accents?' Mike asked, although we weren't expecting anyone to be at the property. 'Just in case?'

'Lincolnshire?' I suggested. 'Isn't that where you're from?'

'I am. You'll just have to do your best. In fact, just say, "Now then," occasionally.'

'Now then,' I practised.

'You'll do.'

We got out of the car and Mike opened the boot, where he stood for a while, hands on hips. I watched, puzzled, as he tore several pages out of an A4 pad, then chose a black rucksack and shoved the pages into it. He closed the boot and locked the car.

'Let's pretend I'm here to pick up some papers?' he said.

'OK.'

'Ah, almost forgot. Names.' He looked at me, with my bouncy ponytail and cap, neat jeans, and navy long-sleeved top. 'How about Heather for you?'

'And maybe Carl for you? With a C.'

Mike nodded. 'Carl and Heather it is.'

'Or even Heather and Carl.'

'Whatever.'

We walked along the short drive that led to the gorgeous old honey-stoned house. From this approach, there was no sign at all of a storage and haulage business, and I guessed all that was hidden behind their very pleasant home and pretty garden.

When a woman appeared at the door, I gasped.

'We'll be fine,' said Mike.

The woman, was young, blonde, and skinny, and struggling to hold back a golden retriever as she came closer.

'Jasper, no!' she said, tugging at the dog's collar while smiling at her visitors. 'Can I help you?' she called out.

'Hey, nice doggy!' said Mike, speeding up. He went over, bent down, and courageously stroked the animal's head, then looked up at the woman. 'We're just here to pick up some paperwork from our storage unit.'

'Ah,' she said. 'The designated entrance to the storage business is off the Witney road.' She pointed behind her and the house.

'I know, sorry. I was hoping Jerry might be home, so we parked up on the road here. Wanted to say a quick hello. I'm Carl, by the way, and this is my partner, Heather.'

'Lucy,' she told us. 'I'm Jerry's son's girlfriend.'

'Jamie?'

'Yes. I'm afraid Jerry's away. They all are. Gone down to their holiday home.'

'Oh, that's a shame. Can't blame them, mind. It'll be smashing down in Bournemouth this weekend. Left you dog sitting, have they?'

'Yeah, just call me Cinders.'

I stood beside Mike and smiled at her. 'We were hoping to see Jerry because we've stupidly forgotten our passcode to get into the main storage building. Well, Carl has.' I gave his shoulder a gentle whack. 'Men, eh? We know the code for the lock on our personal unit, though.'

During the pregnant pause I'd left, Mike gave me a startled you-have-done-your-homework look.

'Sorry, love,' he said, falling into his role. 'Thought I'd written it in my phone. We'll have to come back another time.'

'No, no need,' Lucy said. 'I can let you into the building itself. We have our own passcode.'

'If you're sure?' he said. 'That would be grand.'

'I'll get Jasper indoors and see you out the back.' She pointed to the path we should take around the side of the house.

'Now then,' I said, already setting off. 'Come along, Carl.'

'You're enjoying this, aren't you?' he whispered once abreast.

'I am.'

The house had been extended in every direction, but tastefully. No brash new Cotswold stone, but smooth and stylish limestone with lots of glass that occasionally gave views of the interior. The décor wasn't to my taste – too much heavy oak and pine – but it was evident that the Peacocks were running a profitable business.

'It's rather nice,' I whispered.

'Want to live here?'

'Yes! But then again, no. Not really. Too remote.'

We soon reached the long two-storey building, announcing itself as "Peacock's Self-Service Storage" in large lime-green letters. Nearby stood a neatly parked row of removals vans in matching lettering and colour. Mike was staring at something – a camera up on the wall aimed at the building's wide metal garage-door-type entrance. Next to it was the keypad I'd read about online.

'No windows,' Mike whispered. 'Shit.'

'How do you know Jerry?' Lucy called out from behind.

Mike spun around. 'Rotary Club. He was very good to me when we first moved down from Yorkshire. Gave me lots of useful advice about the area.'

'Yes, Jerry's like that. Really friendly and helpful.'

We stood in front of the opening, and Lucy reminded us that the door would automatically close after forty seconds. 'You definitely know your unit number and the padlock code?'

'We do,' I said, for the first time wondering what the hell we were doing. What if she came in with us? What if you had to use your private unit code to get out again?

Sweat beaded on Mike's brow, and I thought seriously of abandoning the project. And, honestly, what were the chances of finding Hugh anywhere on the premises?

'To reopen the door when you're ready to leave,' said Lucy, 'just press the large green button, inside to the left.'

'Yes, I remember,' I told her.

'Remind me,' said Mike, 'do mobile phones work in there? My mother passed away recently and I need some of her details. Might have to call my brother to check I've got the right papers.'

'Yes, your phones should work. Sorry to hear about your mother.' Lucy strode towards the keypad and Mike hurriedly followed. As she tapped in the code, I watched him either taking a photo of her, or video.

What the fuck? I mouthed, then heard the swoosh of a text being sent. My own phone promptly pinged, just as we stepped inside, and Lucy left us to it. Before I knew it, there was a loud clonking and the huge door shuddered to a thumping close behind us.

Side by side, we stared ahead to the long row of bright-green padlocked doors. I looked up and around at the low polystyrene-tiled ceiling and guessed there was access to another floor somewhere. Were we going to check every unit for Hugh? All two or three hundred?

I turned to Mike, whose face had turned a shade somewhere between white and the green of the doors. An eerie, 'Aaurgh,' came out of his mouth and his legs were jerking oddly.

'What?' I cried as his knees went lower. 'What's the matter? Mike? Are you having a stroke? Oh, Jesus. Mike, get up! Why are you kneeling on the floor? Stop making that noise! Is it your heart? A seizure? No? What are you trying to tell me? The green button? Yes? You want me to press it and open the door? OK.'

I turned and dashed over to the button and bashed it with the palm of my hand. When the door cranked itself upwards again, and the outdoors appeared, Mike got up on shaking legs and wobble-walked outside. I followed him, obviously concerned but not quite suppressing an anxious laugh.

'Claustrophobia?' I asked.

'Yes. Sorry. Better now.' He took a deep breath and exhaled. 'It always passes quickly.'

He did look better. Back had come the summer tan behind the sweatiness. He looked around him, and over to the house.

'Why don't you go in?' he asked, but then the huge green door noisily lowered itself and it was too late. 'I sent you the code,' he added.

I looked back at the house. 'What if she's watching? We can't now use the code that we're not supposed to know.'

'Yeah, you're right. And I'm pretty sure Hugh's not hanging out in that gulag of a place.'

'Me too.' I lowered my voice. 'But he might be camped out in one of the trucks?'

'Or imprisoned in one.'

'Maybe they left Lucy behind to feed him?'

'But Zara would be mad to report him missing, if he was here. Unless she doesn't know.' Mike slung his bag over a shoulder and straightened himself up. He seemed back to normal. 'We could do with Emily and her sixth sense.'

'Everything OK?' shouted Lucy from the back door of the house. Again, she was struggling with the dog.

'Yes, thanks!' I told her.

Mike opened his rucksack and pulled out the pages. 'Took no time to find them!'

'Oh, good! Bye then!'

Mike gave her a thumbs up, and she reversed herself and the dog into the house.

'Would you like me to drive?' I asked as we walked back along the path.

'Would you mind?' he said, handing me the key. 'Sorry.'

'No problem.'

EIGHT

I tried to keep busy to curb my Billy jitters. After a light breakfast in the hotel restaurant, I went back to my room and Skyped Australia. Only Mum was at home.

'Your sister's jogging,' she said.

Jess spent an inordinate amount of her free time running. Since she lived with our mother, two lively child-replacement Labs, and an irritable husband, and ran a kid's clothing business from her dining table, the running made sense.

When Mum asked how I was, I told her we had a new case and gave a sketchy description. But, as usual when I spoke about my business, Mum gently shook her head and asked if I'd considered teaching full-time again. 'Not just dipping in when it suits you.'

I laughed off her question, knowing she was only worried about my safety. Or that was what I chose to believe. She'd absolutely loved telling people when I'd studied at Oxford, and she'd been extremely happy telling them I was a teacher. But now, according to Jess, she tells everyone her youngest daughter runs her own legal firm.

I steered the conversation towards her favourite subject, Alfie, and let her talk at length about him and the things he'd come out with.

'I was so looking forward to seeing him out here at Christmas, but now Maeve's saying she doesn't think they'll make it.'

'Oh?' I'd known about the planned trip and had seriously thought of flying out to Melbourne too. Mum and Jess had last come to the UK over a year ago. 'Do you know why?'

Mum grinned and bobbed her eyebrows. 'She said she'd explain soon.'

'Interesting,' I said. Now my eyebrows joined in, reminding me that I should work on them before my date.

'You don't think…'

Had I seen any signs of pregnancy while I'd been in Brighton? Maeve had put on a little weight, but that could have been down to the bacon baps and Jack's nice dinners.

'Let's not tempt fate,' Mum said, holding up two sets of crossed fingers.

We talked about our approaching autumn and their approaching spring, then we ended the call with blown kisses and the promise not to leave it so long next time.

'You could always Skype me?' I suggested, knowing that would never happen. I'd always been her second-favourite child. Out of two.

Luckily, although he'd never have admitted it, I'd been my dad's favourite. He'd taught me chess, how to swim, and how to make a bow and arrow and balsa wood aeroplanes. He'd created a shortened set of golf clubs for me and given me twenty pence for every lost ball I found during our rounds of nine holes. During our quality time together, Dad would tell me about the cases he was working on, and would sweetly listen to my input when there was one they couldn't solve. At around the age of twelve, I lost interest in golf and chess and policework and generally didn't want to be seen with my dad. It had broken his heart. And now it broke mine, just thinking about it. I shook away the memories and set off for town with a heavy heart – not because of Dad, but because I had to go clothes shopping.

I went for black. A sleeveless black top and black skinny jeans. I found some emerald-coloured dangly earrings and two pretty bangles to add colour, along with a dusty-pink jacket, in case it was cold when the gig finished.

I imagined Billy would come back to the hotel to stay, and having felt depressed by the sight of my Einstein in the various changing-room mirrors, I popped into Boots and bought some straightening tongs.

After taxiing myself back to the hotel, I spent the last half of the afternoon trying to meditate and, after a shower, to smooth my hair without setting it alight, all the while trying not to feel overly anxious about a man I'd only just met. To calm down, I pictured him having some off-putting habit – picking food out of his teeth or a hideous way of dressing for a night out. What if he turned up in white skinny jeans, slip-on shoes and no socks?

At half six, and all ready to go, I hurried down to the bar to wait for him and hopefully fit in a quick drink before he arrived.

However, the lift doors opened to reveal Billy already in the hotel foyer, looking top-to-toe gorgeous, hands in his trouser pockets, brown eyes twinkling at me. I sashayed over, kissed him, then took his hand and led him back into the lift.

* * *

An hour or so later, after I'd quickly showered again and re-ironed my hair, we set off on foot for the Cowley Road.

In a Lebanese restaurant, close to my office, Billy told me more about his marriage break up with his ex-wife, who'd left him for an investment banker, then hadn't been able to cope with their teenage son and the animosity between him and his stepfather.

'He's been with me since he was fourteen,' Billy said.

'Wow. Did he carry on seeing his mum?'

'Yeah, when pushed, but not her husband – not for years. I'd occasionally go off for the weekend so she and Noah could hang out at our house. I, er, had a girlfriend, so the arrangement sort of suited us all.'

'What happened to…'

'The girlfriend?'

'She wanted children,' he said. 'I didn't.'

'Ah.'

'We also had political differences.'

I pulled a face. 'Yeah, that can be a dealbreaker.' I thought of Greg and his views on single-parent benefit scroungers. I'd once screamed back, 'What about the fathers who've fucked off and abandoned their children!' That had been towards the end, when I'd stopped caring. 'Shrill', he'd called me.

'You OK?' asked Billy, reaching across and touching my arm.

'Yes. I'm very OK.'

He smiled and withdrew his hand. 'Not always good to look back, is it?'

God, he was nice. He looked great too. No white skinnies, just black jeans, a grey shirt, greyish-black shoes and, yes, socks. There'd been quite a bit of black between

us, I'd realised in the hotel, so I'd changed into the dress –
now known as my lucky dress – that I'd been wearing
when I'd first bumped into him. I carried the new jacket
and had my phone, room card and debit card inside a small
velvety bag slung across my body.

I insisted we went Dutch, then waited outside while
Billy popped to the loo. I saw I'd missed a call from
Maeve, so texted her, "Sorry! Off to Ben's gig. You OK?"

"I'm jealous", she wrote back. She'd got to know Ben
during our first big case. "Give Emily my love?"

I said I would and wanted to add "I'm on a date!" –
with relevant emojis – but then she'd have phoned again,
and I'd have had to ignore her call. I'd wait until, or if,
Billy and I became more established to tell her.

Glancing up from my phone, I caught Billy looking
around for me on the busy street. I waved and shouted,
'Billy!'

There was no response.

I waved again, and this time tried, 'Ben!'

He quickly spun around and came over. Had he really
not heard me the first time?

'Don't you like me calling you Billy?' I asked. 'It's only
because you look like–'

'I love it,' he said, taking my hand as we walked off.

* * *

There was a decent-sized crowd in the Oxford Scholar,
and as Emily had predicted, I definitely didn't feel old. I
waved at Gary, who was at a table with, presumably, his
wife Stella. He was lifting a pint of Guinness, and Stella
had her fingers in her ears, perhaps not keen on the warm-
up DJ's choice of loud dance tracks.

'My builder!' I shouted at Billy. 'And the woman on the
dance floor is my friend Astrid.' He couldn't miss her,
since she was the only one dancing. She wore almost
exactly what I'd planned to. And with her sleek blonde

hair, and annoying black-clad slimness, I'd definitely have felt like the frumpy dress-alike friend.

'She's doing your kitchen?' he asked.

'Yes!'

We'd reached the bar, where I squeezed into a small space and waved my bank card at the two bartenders.

'Hey, Edie,' yelled Emily, suddenly beside me. 'Thanks for coming!'

I gave her a hug. 'Good crowd already. What would you like to drink?'

'Can I get a Coke?' She pulled a purse from her bag, and I gestured for her to put it back.

'I'm like sooo nervous,' she shouted in my ear.

'He'll be great!' I did a reassuring thumbs up, then put a hand on Billy's shoulder. 'This is Billy, by the way.'

'Oh!' Emily said, wide-eyed.

'Emily,' I told him. I was already losing my voice from shouting over the music, but hoped red wine would help.

'Ah!' he shouted. 'The clever one.'

I ordered the drinks, then the three of us took them to the last free table – the one closest to the loos. There was no point in trying to talk, so I tapped my foot and watched Astrid stabbing the air and twirling her hips.

I couldn't help notice Billy was watching her too. And at one point, when he noticed me watching him watching her, he grinned. 'Not my type, don't worry!' he shouted.

'I wasn't worrying!'

He pulled a sceptical face and squeezed my hand.

'Aw,' said Emily, beside me.

The Off Beats came on to much applause and tuned their guitars. Ben introduced the band. 'Two of us are coppers, so all you underage drinkers switch to lemonade or you'll get the landlord closed down. And we don't want that, do we?'

'No!' we all shouted.

I looked around and saw no one under eighteen, or anywhere near it. They'd be arriving later, I imagined, full of out-of-date corner-shop cider.

Across the room, Stella had taken her fingers out of her ears, and within a few drumbeats and accompanying guitar chords, she and Gary were up and grooving with Astrid. While Gary jerkily dad danced and Stella did a lot of arm flapping, I began to panic. When had I last danced? Could I still? And if I couldn't but Billy really could, would he decide that was it? Would it be our dealbreaker? 'We had dancing differences,' he'd explain to the next girlfriend.

'They're really good!' I shouted to Emily, who was anxiously watching the door, where a few people, who I guessed had only come for the DJ, were drifting out of the pub.

As they left, in walked Mike. While he made his way through the crowd, he talked over his shoulder to the person behind him; a slim, good-looking, dark-haired guy in his late twenties or early thirties. At the bar, while they waited to be served, the friend put his arm around Mike's waist. Wait, what? Mike?

'What's the matter?' asked Emily.

I nodded towards Mike. 'Is Mike… you know?

'What, gay? Of course he is! Edie, you're hilarious sometimes.'

'I know,' I said. I was beginning to realise that when Emily called me funny or hilarious, she meant unobservant or not quite getting it. Hardly the best traits in my line of work.

Billy said, 'What's funny?'

'Edie didn't realise–'

'Come on!' I said, jumping up and giving her a 'Don't!' scowl. 'Let's all dance?'

Thankfully, I remembered how to, and as more people joined us, waving and swaying in an appropriately hippy way to the jingly-jangly guitar and keyboard sounds of the sixties, only with an added grungy edge, I began to relax and enjoy myself. Mike came over and introduced his friend as Seth, and the two of them launched into some punchy manspreading moves.

When Billy pulled me closer, in either a protective or proprietorial way, we slow danced for a bit, and as the room and the music and the faces spun around us, I became aware of a throbbing by my hip.

'Is that you or my mobile?' I asked Billy. He laughed and said what did I think he was, sixteen?

We moved apart so I could get my phone out. A missed call. "Jessica", it said. She hadn't left a voicemail message, but a text popped up. "Where are you?"

"Oxford Scholar, Cowley Road", I typed back. "Band playing. Come and join us?"

A bit forward, I realised, considering Jessica was a client, but I couldn't unsend it.

Between songs we went back to the bar, where I checked my phone again. Still no response from Jessica, who was probably now seeing me as totally unprofessional. Hey ho, I thought, swiftly distracted by Billy asking which red wine I wanted.

Another song started up and I watched Emily dancing with a group of friends, her eyes on Ben. Then, just as Billy handed me my wine, a familiar face loomed up and said, 'Hello, Edie. Long time no shee.'

'Hey!' I shouted. 'How are you?' It was Emily's dad, Steve. He hadn't changed too much and even had the same long hair, only now it was a greyish blond and around an eighth of its old thickness.

'I have to tell you, Edie, how very proud of Emily we are. After all she went through with that bastard Toby, and then the four lots of rehab.'

'Four?' I said.

'It nearly bankrupted us, but look at how she's turned out. A heart of gold and good career prospects. That's partly down to you, Edie, and I'd like to thank you, deeply,

deeply, from the bottom of our hearts. Mine and um…
er…'

'Linda's?' Steve was clearly drunk as a skunk, and I
managed to sidestep a grateful hug. 'Emily's a star,' I said.
'Couldn't run the place without her.'

'And she'll be even more useful to you once she passes
this driving test.'

'She will!' Emily was learning to drive? I had no idea.
No doubt she'd call me hilarious.

'She's refusing to tell her mum and me when the test is,
only that it's very, very soon.'

'I could sense Billy was feeling left out, or maybe I just
felt he was being left out, so I hooked a reassuring arm
through his.

Steve frowned and took a swig of beer. Had he really
once been a lecturer? He'd packed it in to go off grid and
mess up his daughter's life. Mind you, it was touching to
hear how proud he was of her now.

Emily herself appeared beside us and led her dad away,
mouthing, 'Sorry,' over her shoulder. Then the band struck
up again, and Billy nudged me.

'Are you wanting to dance some more?' I asked.

'Uh uh.' He nodded to the entrance, where a woman
with messy dark hair, a white face, and mascara-smudged
eyes stood staring at me. Jessica? Every time I saw her she
looked different. I hurried over, dragging Billy with me.

'Are you OK?' I asked.

'They've found Hugh,' she said. 'He's—'

Her face contorted, her eyes rolled up, and her body
crumpled to the floor. A woman nearby screamed, and the
band, one by one, stopped playing.

NINE

We'd all taken Monday off to recover from Sunday evening and the news that Hugh had been found dead. 'A breather,' I'd called it during our brief early-morning video call.

'Unlike poor Hugh,' Mike had said and laughed, then Emily called him disrespectful and hung up.

'Death affects people differently,' said Mike, then he too was gone.

We were supposed to all meet at the office at two today, but instead, I found myself at my desk at quarter to two, sitting opposite a sobbing Jessica and an unexpected Ben. When Emily burst through the door behind them, beaming, my guests turned their heads her way.

'Guess what!' she said.

'You passed your driving test?' I asked.

'I did! But how did you... Oh God, Jessica. I'm like sooo sorry.' She unhooked her cloth bag and gave Jessica and her wodge of wet tissue a hug, then came and sat beside me.

'That's fantastic news,' I said quietly. I glanced over at the other office, indicating Mike was in there.

Emily nodded. 'Thanks,' she whispered. 'First time, can't believe it.'

'Is it OK to start now?' asked Ben. 'Only, I do have my own cases.'

'Please do,' I told him.

'Once again,' he said, 'I'm sorry for your loss, Jessica. Are you going to be all right with this?'

'Yes.'

'DS Laing is indisposed today with a personal matter, so I thought I'd come and bring you all here at Fox Wilder up to date.' He looked at Jessica again. 'If you'd rather, I could drive you home and come back?'

'I'll be OK.'

Ben referred to a notebook. 'Hugh was last seen, as far as we know, on Friday, 14 August, at the home of Jerry and Fiona Peacock near the village of Fellford in West Oxfordshire. He'd gone to spend a few days there with the Peacocks' daughter, Zara.' Ben glanced at Jessica, then went on. 'It seems he and Zara had a row during the first evening. Around nine o'clock he said he was going for a walk and told Zara not to wait up for him. Which she didn't.'

Emily put her hand up. 'Has this all come from Zara, or did her parents say the same?'

'Jerry and Fiona Peacock confirmed what Zara said, yes. When Hugh hadn't come back by the next morning, Zara guessed he'd either gone back to her flat in Summertown or to one of the friends he often went to see or stay with. Zara knew he had cash at that point because she'd provided it. He bought and sold things, apparently. He'd even sold his car.'

Jessica made a strange noise behind the tissues.

'Due to being overdrawn on his own bank account, payments from the sold items went into Zara's account, and she gave him the cash and some extra.'

'I take it she tried calling him?' I asked.

'Let me see... sorry, these aren't my notes. Um, yeah, here we are. Hugh had stopped using his own phone a few weeks before going missing and had been getting by with Zara's mum's old non-smartphone. However, he'd left that behind at the Peacocks' house in his "hurry to flounce off", as Zara put it when she reported him missing last week. His not having a decent working smartphone had been a pain, but Zara said she'd understood why he'd stopped using his usual one.'

'Because...?' I asked.

'Apparently, he didn't want to be found by… well, you, Jessica.'

'Why was that?' she asked.

'Because, according to Zara, he was afraid that once you found him, you'd be able to divorce him. And because of the prenup… excuse me, postnup, he'd be left with, to quote Zara quoting Hugh, "Eff all after everything I've done for her and her kids". When the bod– When Hugh was found' – Ben flicked through some pages – 'on the western edge of Hilltop Woods by a trespassing dog walker last Thursday, nobody knew who he was because of the state Hugh was in, which I won't describe now, but there'd been some decom–'

Jessica sobbed.

'Sorry,' he said. 'Anyway, it was several days before Hugh was identified from dental records, and we only learned about the find at Cowley station on Sunday morning. When DS Laing couldn't get hold of you, Jessica, Hugh was formally identified at the John Radcliffe by his parents, and then DS Laing and DC Lisa Patel immediately came to notify you. But I believe you'd already heard from Mr and Mrs Horsfield by then?'

'Yes,' she whispered.

'Owing to a bit of a backlog, we're still waiting for the forensic pathologist's report for confirmation of cause of death. I'm not sure if DS Laing told you, Jessica, but Hugh was found beside a paper bag with a couple of magic mushrooms inside it. We've assumed he was out foraging for them, perhaps in the fields surrounding the woods.'

'What? No, no, that can't be right.' Jessica jumped up and paced around the room. 'It doesn't make sense. Hugh might have messed around with such things when he was younger, I mean who didn't?' She scratched her head and occasionally sniffed. 'Unless this double life of his with Zara, together with the stress of our marriage failing… I mean, he's always been impressionable and a little insecure…' She wiped away a new tear.

Ben closed his notepad and stood up. 'Once again, I'm so sorry for your loss. As I said, we'll know more soon. I'm afraid I have another appointment to get to but if you have any questions, do email or call me, or leave it until tomorrow when DS Laing should be back in. He or I will keep you updated, Jessica.'

I got up and walked to the door with him. 'Thank you for stepping in for DS Laing and coming to see us.'

'You're welcome,' he said. 'Oh, and we'd be grateful if you'd keep this to yourselves. There'll be a press release in due course, but we've already had a local reporter sniffing around.'

'Of course.'

'Just one more question,' said Emily. She had her arm in the air but slowly lowered it. 'Do you know if Zara's brother Jamie was there that Friday evening?'

'Or his girlfriend Lucy?' I added.

Ben pulled out the notebook again and flicked through. 'Yes, they both were. They were interviewed too, and they confirmed what Zara and her parents said.'

Emily smiled at her boyfriend, who'd not, as far as I could tell, yet made eye contact with her. 'OK,' she said. 'Thanks, Detective Sergeant.'

'You're welcome.' He finally looked at her and smiled back. 'And congratulations on the test.'

'The reason I dropped by,' said Jessica, once Ben had left, 'was to settle up with you.'

'Oh?' I said, taken aback.

'But first, may I use your loo?'

'Of course.'

'I'll show you where it is,' Emily said.

While they were gone, I popped my head around Mike's door and whispered, 'Blimey.'

'Ditto,' he whispered back. 'Good of Ben to come and tell us. I don't suppose the other DS would have.'

'No.' I quickly checked the office over my shoulder. 'If it looks as though she'll be here a while, we'll take her next door for a coffee.'

'OK.'

When I heard the toilet on the landing flush. I retreated to my office, leaving the door ajar.

Back on her chair and miraculously glammed up but still red-eyed, Jessica asked how much she owed us. 'Now that Hugh's been found, I guess I won't need your services from here on.'

'If anything, we owe you.'

'Goodness, no.'

Emily was tapping her phone on her chin. I'd come to see it as a sign she was thinking great thoughts. 'So, you're not suspicious?' she asked. 'You don't think Hugh was like…'

'Obviously it's crossed my mind,' said Jessica. 'But who'd have had a motive?'

'What about Zara?' Emily persisted. 'What if he said he was leaving her that evening?'

Jessica rubbed at one temple with her fingertips. 'I suppose it's possible that someone was the cause of Hugh's… demise. Whether inadvertently or not. God, I still can't believe it.' She shook her head and got out another tissue. 'But let's give the police time to work out the cause of… I mean, if it looks suspicious, surely they'll be onto it immediately?'

'I guess so,' I said. 'So, for now, is there anything we can be doing? You did pay for a week's work, and we're not there yet.'

'I can't really think what, but thank you. And thank you for, well, listening. You've both been great, and perhaps we could meet up again, if I'm in Oxford, or if you're in my neck of the woods?'

'Of course,' I said, trying to think if I'd ever been in Primrose Hill's neck of the woods. Only once, I remembered, on top of the hill itself with its wonderful views of London.

Jessica stood up and checked her watch. 'I'm heading back home shortly. I've broken the news to the boys, and they're distraught, poor loves.' She held out a hand and I shook it, and with an effusive and watery eyed 'Thank you both so much', she left.

* * *

Once we'd heard the door to the shop downstairs firmly close and I'd watched her leave the building through the window, Mike emerged from his room. We all sat silently shell-shocked for a while.

'Do you still want me to fix Toby's window?' Mike asked Emily.

'Did you buy the materials?'

'No. I've been a bit preoccupied, what with Seth staying. He left today, so now I'm all yours.'

Emily chin tapped. 'Actually, yeah, let's not bother fixing it. The window's hidden behind this like cruddy, smelly old curtain, so knowing Toby, he'll forget all about it.'

'If you're sure?' said Mike. 'I've got quite a bit of teaching, so that suits me. But if he makes a fuss, let me know.'

'Cheers, I will.' Emily looked my way. 'You OK, Edie?'

'Yeah, yeah. Just need to get my head around everything.'

'Here's a suggestion,' said Mike. 'Let's wait until the cause of Hugh's death is known. Presumably, Ben will tell you, Em?'

'He'd better!' Emily said.

Mike smiled. 'Then we'll get together again, air our thoughts, and decide if we need to do anything further, client or no client.'

'OK,' I said. 'But first we should tell Emily about our trip to Fellford.'

Emily looked at us. 'You both went?'

'We did,' I said. 'Mike heard in Zara's café that the Peacock family, including Zara and Jamie, had gone away to their holiday home on the coast, so at the last minute he decided to come with me. Lucy, Jamie's girlfriend was there dog sitting.'

Emily nodded. 'Ah, that's how you knew about her.'

'We thought we'd take a look around the storage units, however…' I grimaced Mike's way.

'Edie's dying to tell you I had a massively wimpy attack of claustrophobia inside the building.'

'No windows?' asked Emily.

Mike grimaced. 'None.'

'Urgh, that's like the worst. Toby locked me in his great-gran's old trunk once. You know, like they used to have in the olden days before wheelie cases?'

'He *what*?' asked Mike.

'All cos I'd like accidentally thrown away some black bag he'd stashed some drugs in? Binmen took it. Yeah, can't even go in a lift now.'

'Christ, that man should be in prison,' I said. 'Speaking of which, did you talk to Ben about–'

'Wow, is that the time?' she said, looking at our clock. It was deliberately placed on the wall behind the clients' seats to save me rudely checking the time on my phone or watch. Emily got up and made for the door. 'Got to get an assignment submitted today.'

After her sudden departure, Mike and I agreed there wasn't anything we could do for now, so we left the office and its strange atmosphere and quietly parted out on the street. After the drama and heightened emotions of the past few days, it all felt horribly anticlimactic.

TEN

I'd been woken at eight in the morning. by a text from Emily. She had some news, so all three of us were now in the office.

'Go on,' I said, bracing myself. It had actually been very pleasant yesterday, not thinking about all this and what we should do next, if anything. I'd begun to consider going back to Brighton and catching the last days of summer, but an image of Billy finding another lost woman quashed that idea.

'So, cause of death...' said Emily, reading from her phone. 'Was... amatoxin poisoning, caused by ingesting Amanita phalloides.' She looked up at us. 'The police think he accidentally ate some death cap mushrooms. Or even just one, which is enough to kill you.'

'While out picking magic mushrooms?' asked Mike. 'Does that make sense? You take them home and dry them out for several days before eating them. Er, so I'm told.'

'Ha ha, Mike. Yeah, it is a bit odd, but Ben said the contents of Hugh's stomach proved he'd eaten both types of mushrooms the day before he died. He'd had mushroom soup as well, with the usual kind of mushrooms in it. So, that made it three types! Talk about confusing. Anyway, maybe Hugh was out looking for more of the magic kind when he began to feel like shit. Death cap takes like six to twelve hours to kick in. Then they do this evil stuff to you. Have a look on Wikipedia.'

Mike and I googled the symptoms on my laptop. It would indeed be a ghastly way to go. Vomiting, diarrhoea, severe abdominal pain, liver and kidney failure. We also learned that the spores of death cap mushrooms are easily transferred and need extremely high temperatures to destroy them.

'That bit's seriously scary,' said Mike.

'Yep. It'll make me think twice about taking the grandkids on a country walk.'

'Or the dog?'

'Or the dog.'

I got up an image of a death cap, and then one of a magic mushroom, Latin name psilocybin. 'Is it me,' I asked, 'or does the death cap look nothing like the magic?'

'Not even the smaller baby death cap would pass as a magic mushroom,' said Mike. 'It's more yellow, not pointed.'

Emily came and peered at my screen. 'Maybe if you were in a dark forest or wood, you might not be able to tell?'

'I'm not sure they grow in woods,' said Mike. 'My friends always went to fields to find them.'

Emily smirked. 'Is that right?'

'But you'd surely notice once you got it home,' I said. 'Did Ben tell you where Hugh had been staying? Was it near this Hilltop Woods?'

'They reckon it was in a sort of groundsman's brick hut in the woods that had been boarded up recently. Found some of his things there. They've had forensics go over it and found traces of mushrooms, although not death cap, so far. Ben said it's like basically one room with a camp bed, a camping stove, a sink, and a loo in a cupboard. You know, maybe it didn't have proper lighting?'

'This is all on the Warlops' estate,' said Mike, still scribbling.

'Who are they?' I asked.

'They own Warlop House, Hilltop Woods, and a lot besides. I looked it up after Ben came here. An industrialist called Thomas Warlop bought it for a song in the late forties, after the war. Did it up, and liked it so much he retired there. Got a peerage for services to something. The place regularly opens to the public. Has llamas apparently. It's now run by Thomas's granddaughter and husband, or maybe great-granddaughter.'

'And how close is this to the Peacocks in Fellford?'

'It's around three miles from Fellford to the woods and the groundsman's hut, and about four to the main house. The Warlops have a lot of land.'

Mike and I looked at each other, both thinking the same thing.

'We could be Heather and Carl again,' I suggested. 'Unless you'd like to go out there with Mike, Em? Bit of a jaunt?'

'I'd love to, but I've got to do a few things. Plus, I think you're a much better actress than me, Edie.'

'Really?'

'I'd probably say the wrong thing. Open my big mouth!'

There was that.

'So,' she continued, 'as far as I know from Ben, the police are investigating the circumstances of Hugh's death, cos they could be considered suspicious. And, fingers crossed, it just might become Ben's case today. DS Laing is signed off sick. Had a breakdown or something.'

'Oh, that is good news,' I said. 'Not for DS Laing, obviously. Do you think Ben would mind if we did a bit of snooping around?'

'To be honest, I reckon he'd welcome it. They're waiting on a warrant to search Jessica and Hugh's flat in Divinity Road, plus Zara's place in Summertown.'

'I suppose they have to cover everything.' I had a little think, drumming fingers on the desk. 'Are we all OK with this? It's a bit odd not having a client, but are you happy to carry on, Em? Fit it in around your shifts downstairs?'

'Definitely, if it helps Ben. And I should earn my money!'

I paid Emily a weekly retainer, whether or not there was any work for her. But I only paid Mike for the hours he clocked up.

'Mike?'

'Yeah, I'm good with that. I could move a few tutorials around if necessary. You're OK paying me, even though you're not being paid?'

'I am,' I said. Anything was better than having to think about my house. 'Jessica did give us a chunk, and we're nowhere near through it yet.'

Emily left to work in the shop, and Mike and I went back to the hotel to pick up my Heather-wear, then set off for Warlop House and gardens. They closed at half five, which gave us plenty of time to wander around speaking in northern accents.

* * *

'I wonder if we'll find the groundman's place Hugh stayed in?' I said once we were going west along the A40.

'If we do, you won't catch me going in.'

'Because it'll be contaminated with death cap? I hadn't thought of that. Got any masks in this dressing room on wheels? Rubber gloves?'

'I do, funnily enough. No, I'm not scared of a little death cap. But a boarded-up building? No, thanks.'

We didn't go directly to Warlop House, but skirted the estate and, with the aid of my phone, found ourselves driving past Hilltop Woods. At one point we'd seen a sign to Fellford, where the Peacocks lived, telling us it was three and a half miles away. An easy distance for the pissed-off Hugh to have covered on foot that evening. Had he known about the hut? Used it before to hide from his women, or even take them there?

At the main entrance to the woods – a gated-off dusty dirt road – there were several strands of blue-and-white police tape and a temporary notice we couldn't make out from the road. Closer to us was a 'Private, Keep Out' sign with threats of prosecution.

'I bet the groundsman's cottage isn't far from here,' I said, happy to go and explore, since there were no actual police officers in sight.

'I doubt we'd be able to see in.'

'True.'

We drove along the road around the estate, then through the gates that led to Warlop House. Fifty yards in we were stopped beside a wooden building by a middle-aged, suit-wearing woman with a card reader in her hand. The current owner mucking in? I wondered.

She asked for an astonishing fifty pounds.

'I'll get it, Carl,' I said, leaning across him to tap my business debit card and taking the two scrappy little tickets she held out. I examined them, back and front, as we pulled away.

Mike glanced over. 'I take it we get a free llama ride for that?'

'You'd think.'

'A cup of tea?'

'No, but the tiny print at the bottom says we have free entry for a year.' Thinking I could bring Alfie to see the llamas, I tucked them in my purse for safekeeping.

As we followed signs to the car park, I took in Warlop House, where a grey-haired man behind a table at the main entrance appeared to be taking money for a flimsy guide. What a cash cow this place was.

'Don't tell me,' said Mike as we inched towards the overflow car park. 'You want to live here.'

'Christ, no.'

'Why not?'

'Let me think. Heating bills and general upkeep? Dead bodies in the grounds?'

Mike drove another inch, then looked around. 'Nice lawns, though.'

'Very.'

Having finally parked on a bumpy overflow field behind Warlop House, we remained in the car looking at some video and photos Emily had just sent us both.

"Do you know who this is?" her text said. "Was passing Jessica's flat and he pulled up and went in and came out with that big bag and drove off."

'It's Jamie,' said Mike.

'Zara's brother? Are you sure?' Mike had seen Jamie in Zara's café, so he should know. 'What's he doing letting himself into Jessica's place?'

'More importantly,' said Mike, 'what's in the stuffed bag he left with? Jessica's jewellery?'

'More importantly than even that is what's Emily doing blatantly filming him? And why is she in Divinity Road again? Not visiting that awful drug-dealer ex, Toby, I hope.'

I called Emily, but she didn't answer, then filled Mike in on what she'd told me about the young girl he has there. And that he could do violent things.

'Like locking his girlfriend in a trunk?' he asked. 'That's assault and false imprisonment, and I don't know why Em stayed with him.'

I tried her again and it rang out. Was she with Toby getting trashed, her phone on silent?

'Emily was an addict, remember. I hope she's not on a downward trajectory.'

Mike shrugged. 'Nah, we'd have noticed the signs if she was doing drugs. I had a few druggy mates and it's pretty obvious.'

I paused before asking if he'd used, back in the day.

'A bit of weed,' he said. 'Occasional mushrooms, too.' He saw my face. 'Yeah, I know what I said in the office. It was just at uni for the first couple of terms. But I was doing drama and had to memorise lines, so… yeah, wasn't a good mix. Then I got my highs from acting, luckily. I'll text Emily now and tell her it's Jamie.'

Had I actually seen or been offered drugs during my one year at Oxford? I couldn't remember any. Just masses of drinking sessions, one of which led to Maeve being created.

'Edie?' I heard.

'Mm?'

'I said, what if Jamie and Jessica are in cahoots? And maybe Zara too. And then there's Lucy, who's seen us at the Peacocks' place pretending to be Carl and Heather.'

'Oh, right…'

'And we're actually very close to Fellford at the moment, so who knows who could roll up here and recognise us? Not to mention what they might be capable of.'

'I see what you mean.' I looked at the photo of shifty-looking Jamie shoving a bag in the boot of his car. Had he spotted Emily filming him? Bundled her into the car, too?

I tried calling her again and got no response.

'Tell you what,' said Mike. 'Let's get the fuck out of here.'

'Quick,' I told him, buckling up while he reversed out of the parking space. 'Quick.'

'OK, OK.'

ELEVEN

We parked opposite Jessica's flat and stared at it through Mike's tinted windows.

'Do you think Jessica went home?' Mike asked.

'I'm sure she did, what with the twins needing support. We could check?'

'We could.'

'She's never actually seen you, has she? Maybe you could knock on the door while you're still in disguise? Be a Jehovah's Witness?'

Mike laughed. 'Could be dangerous. Jessica might want to hear all about it, pleased to have the company. I did a stint in telesales after uni. Lot of lonely people out there.'

Mike went and tried Jessica's door and was back in seconds. 'No signs of life. The place is in darkness.'

'Could you pop back and listen for Emily's phone ringing? A bit far-fetched, I know, but… I'll try her again.'

'Isn't it always on silent?'

'Only at work. Her ringtone's that old Pink Floyd song about Emily.'

'*See Emily Play*?'

'Ben's favourite song, apparently.'

Once he was by the flat again, I called her. Mike moved to the bay window and cupped a hand to it, shook his head at me and came back to the car.

'Well that's a relief,' I said. Or was it?

Since I was meeting Billy for dinner, I told Mike I'd walk from Jessica's to the office to change. I was supposed to drop in to Billy's place of work, but had quickly texted to say I'd see him at the restaurant instead. I really wasn't in the mood to meet the fabulous Georgia.

With a bit of time to spare, I wandered up Divinity Road to roughly where Toby might live. I hadn't gone far when I spotted Emily's distinctive pink bike leaning against a house behind a wall. The ground-floor bay window was curtained and impossible to see into, and as far as I could tell, it had no broken panes of glass.

I looked up and immediately spotted the damage Emily had done. Was she in there, smoking or snorting? Or worse. Would ringing the doorbell be an intrusion into my employee's privacy, or a genuine act of concern? An intervention. I was torn. Then, before I could talk myself out of it, I rang the bell for Flat 2 and held my breath. There was a speaker-phone, but no one spoke or buzzed me in, so I stepped back onto the pavement and looked up. No one came to the window or the door.

I rang again. And again. Perhaps I'd annoy them into answering.

Of course, the fact that Emily's bike was outside didn't mean she was inside. She, or they, could have gone out – been in a pub or somewhere.

After calling her number once again and hearing her chirpy voicemail instructions. I left a message to let me know if she was OK, then texted her too.

Emily was always prompt to reply, but not this time. I waited a while. Hadn't she taken up yoga? Somewhere off the Cowley Road, I was sure she'd said. She could be there right now with the after-work lot. But wait, what if she'd lost her phone? Maybe in some scuffle with Jamie.

I took out my small handbag notebook and scribbled a quick "Are you OK? Give me a call? Or email? Edie x".

As I leaned across to pop the note in her bike basket, I saw, on the ground, next to the iron ring the bike was locked to – amongst all the sweet wrappers, polystyrene boxes, and last year's dead leaves that had landed behind the wall – a mid-sized terracotta plant pot, half full of dried-out soil. It had a circle of clear space around it, as though it was often moved. Something told me there'd be a key underneath, and when I bent down and lifted it, there was. Two, in fact, on one key ring. Which flat did they belong to, 1 or 2?

I bent down and picked them up, looked over both shoulders, and then did something really stupid. Even more stupid than leaving your keys under a pot on the second-busiest street in east Oxford.

At the top of the grubby, maroon-carpeted stairs was a door that might have once been white. I knocked on it tentatively, then less so, and when no one answered, I put the second key, somewhat shakily, into the lock.

It worked. I counted to the beat of my thumping heart, up to ten, then stepped into an enormous tip of a room.

No one was there. No Emily slumped lifeless over the manky Chesterfield. Habitat? I wondered, vaguely spotting a familiar pattern through the grime. My parents had one the same. Used to have, before my world collapsed, my dad no longer in it.

I went down a short hallway and looked into a smallish bedroom, almost entirely filled with a bed. At the end of the hall was a bathroom with an ancient cast-iron bath and a loo with a chain to pull. The basin contained plants sitting in inches of water, and the windowsill was covered with dusty cacti. On the shelf at the foot of the bath were a hundred burned-down candles on a sea of melted wax. The room smelt surprisingly nice, and the loo was surprisingly clean.

I made use of the facilities, then heard the bang of a door and panicked. I felt sure it had come from the flat downstairs, but not that sure.

I really had to get out of the flat.

But maybe a very quick look around, I thought, back in the living room. The ceiling was high with attractive coving – or were they architraves? I'd ask Gary. Gorgeous ceiling rose, original fireplace and surrounding tiles. Stripped pine doors and floors. Those were the pluses.

The downside was the utter chaos. Sleeping bags, burnt-looking spoons, bits of silver foil and shoes and books and half-eaten bowls of brown stuff, wrappers, and clothes, and large, stained floor cushions. The kitchen area was a mountain of dirty pots, pans, plates, more uneaten food, and a large chef's knife covered in something reddish-brown and shiny.

Please, not Emily's blood.

What a gorgeous flat it could have been though, with its large living-kitchen-dining area – the house's original master bedroom and the middle one must have been knocked through. There were some beautiful Victorian features, many hidden under layers of nicotine-stained paint. Who owned it? Toby himself?

On a relatively uncluttered kitchen worktop, a large envelope caught my eye. It was open and, as far as I could tell, deliberately propped up against a teapot.

Emily – because I knew her handwriting – had jotted down some things. "T's Mum" followed by a mobile number, and underneath was "T's Dad" followed by a mobile number. Below "T's Dad" she'd written "Tim" in brackets, with a circle over the *i*. Definitely Emily then. She'd drawn an arrow towards "T's Dad (Tim)", almost like an instruction.

Had she left the envelope for me? No, crazy idea. A message from the gods, then? I looked up at the ceiling to my own dad. Was this a sign, I asked him, to call the number? When the boiler beside me chose that moment to click and fire up, I took that as a yes.

As I tapped in the number, I felt some relief. If Emily was leaving me notes she must be OK. 'Hello?' I said when a man answered. 'Is that Tim?'

'It is. To whom am I speaking?' He sounded proper but nice, and I relaxed a little.

'My name's Edie Fox. I'm just calling because Emily–'

'Ah, splendid!' he cried. I heard a woman murmur something. 'It's young Emily's boss, dear. Just one moment, Edie, while I put you on the loudspeaker. I'm sure my wife would like to hear what you have to say.'

'Er… OK.'

'There. We were going to give you a ring, but this is fine, and thank you so much for getting in touch first. Now, let me see, where shall we begin. Um, would you say Emily is reliable?'

I blinked, frowned, shook my head, and said, 'Very.'

'And conscientious? Once she commits to something, does she see it through?'

'She does.'

'And most importantly, considering what we have in mind for her, would you say she's honest?'

At that moment I wasn't so sure. 'Scrupulously.'

'That's a relief, isn't it, darling?' I hoped he was talking to his wife. 'I know most of it's just Toby's paraphernalia, but he'll hardly want anyone seeing it, let alone storing it, while he's… how shall I put it… away for a while.'

'No,' I agreed. Did he mean prison? Had Emily actually reported him? I did hope so. I felt myself relax. Oh, but maybe Tim meant abroad. Either way, it seemed Toby wasn't going to turn up any minute.

'However, there might be one or two valuables lying around. Or things of sentimental value.'

'I guarantee she'd let you know, Tim.'

'Excellent.'

'And I've said I'll help,' I threw in, for extra reassurance.

'Ah, splendid. Thank you, Edie. Um, Emily didn't actually mention what kind of business she worked for? What is it you do?'

'Well…' My mother's features swam past my eyes. 'I run a legal firm.'

'How interesting that must be. You're not representing Toby, by any chance? In fact, no, don't answer that. We've decided to stay well clear this time.'

'No, we're not representing him. Anyway, Tim, I'm afraid I'm going to have to–'

'Of course, of course, I expect you're terribly busy. Thank you very much for the reference, Edie.'

'My pleasure.'

When we said goodbye, I stopped pacing around and sat for a while on a grim dining chair, staring into space as I tried to piece it all together. Why would Emily offer to clear out her horrible ex's horrible flat? She'd have her reasons, I knew. Was she selling off any remaining drugs? Getting some recompense for what he'd put her through. Or it could simply be that Tim was paying her well for a job he and his wife couldn't face. Probably the latter.

My increasingly tired eyes landed on something very familiar. It was an abstract oil painting, about three foot high and propped against the wall beside the fireplace. Where had I seen it before? It was recently…

'Shit!' I said. It had been on Jessica's phone – one of the items Hugh had taken when he'd moved out. But how had it ended up in Toby's flat? Had Toby, in fact, known Hugh? Maybe Hugh had settled a debt with the picture?

When the buzzer chose that moment to blast out, my body jolted and my heart began thumping. Oh, but maybe it was Emily. Mind you, she had the set of keys Toby had given her.

I tiptoed to the big bay window and peered around the curtain she'd described perfectly. It was rank. Down below I saw the top of a man's blond head. He buzzed again, then three, four times more. Perhaps Toby was famously slow to get to the door or hard to rouse.

I went and picked up the entry-phone and said, 'Hello?'

'Is Tobes in?' he asked.

'He's out at the moment. I'm not sure when he'll be back.'

Three years?

'Don't suppose you can buzz me in? I just need to drop off some cash. He said he'd break my legs if he didn't get it by today, so…'

'Er…' Obviously I didn't want to let him in, but what kind of person was I dealing with? One who'd lurk outside and attack me?

'I'll be a minute tops.'

'OK,' I said, pressing the buzzer, then opening the flat door. As I watched the blond head take the stairs two at a time, I realised it belonged to none other than Jamie.

'Hi,' I said, when he got to the door and stepped inside the flat.

'Hi, I'm Jamie.'

'I'm… actually just here to inspect a broken window. Toby gave my assistant keys to let ourselves in.'

'Really? That's uncharacteristically trusting of him.' He went over to the kitchen and took a large Italian biscuit tin from a shelf above the sink. 'That's weird,' he said, shoving a rolled wad of notes in. 'It's never usually empty.'

'You look familiar,' I told him. 'Have we met before?'

He tilted his head and took in my face. 'I get this a lot. Have you ever been to Nice Buns in Headington?'

'Ah, that's it. You work there, don't you?'

'Yeah, just temporarily. Helping my sister out while she's going through some stuff. She owns it.'

'Oh, Zara?'

'You know her, do you?'

'Kind of.'

'And do you know about–'

'Hugh? Yes, I heard. Awful.'

'Tragic,' said Jamie, shaking his head, hands on hips. 'We'd become good mates.'

'Oh, I'm sorry.' I was still tense but keen to find out more. 'Um, would you like a cup of tea or something? Coffee?' Christ, what was I doing? I instantly wanted him to say no and crossed two sets of fingers.

Jamie looked back at the kitchen. 'I think that might be living dangerously. I could make you one over the road, though. If you like.'

I relaxed a little but was torn. If he'd done something to Emily, was I going to be next? But if he knew something that would help explain Hugh's death, I should, as a professional investigator, follow it up.

'Is that where you live?' I asked.

'It's where Hugh lived, actually. Belongs to his wife, Jessica.'

OK, the moment had come to come clean. 'I actually know Jessica, too.' I opened my bag and took out a card. 'She's my client.'

* * *

Jessica's front room was cosy and classy. Lots of books, a Turkish rug, a deep blue comfy sofa, and two modern leather armchairs, one of which Jamie sat in. He was drinking white wine he said he'd found in the fridge, and since he'd already opened the bottle, I said yes to a glass. It was very nice, but then Jessica would know her wines.

It was funny how Jamie's sister was pretty, at least in the photos online, but the same features didn't suit a man. He was what my mum would call lanky; tall, skinny, and probably didn't work out.

'Hugh's death was a bit of a shocker for all of his mates,' he said, with his left ankle resting on his right knee.

'I bet.'

'An accident, they say. The police.'

'I think they're still investigating.'

'You mean they suspect foul play?'

I shrugged. 'It's a strange way of saying "murder", isn't it? Makes it sound like a misdemeanour on the rugby pitch.'

Jamie looked shocked, and his left foot began jiggling. 'So you think they might think it was murder?'

'I've no idea what they think. We'll just have to wait and see what they come up with.'

'Or who,' he said.

'So, you knew Hugh quite well, it seems. How about Jessica? Did you ever meet her?'

Jamie stared at me, his foot jiggling faster. 'Er, I might have… although I can't quite…' He put his glass down and got up, then went out to the hall and returned with a small pouch. Back in the armchair, he took out a Rizla paper. 'Shit,' he said quietly, then, 'Fuck, fuck, fuck. All my fault.' He looked up and started, as though he'd forgotten I was there.

'What's all your fault?' Was he about to confess to something? In which case I should record it. I pulled my phone out, eyes trained on his face.

'What?' he asked, heating a lump of hash with a lighter. 'Oh, right, yeah. It's just that Hugh asked me to come here and pick something up for him, and I never did, not till today. Too late.'

'Do you mind telling me what?'

He slowly finished making his spliff, then drew on it and held the smoke it. 'Books,' he wheezed, breathing out. He pointed at the top bookshelves that ran either side of the chimney breast. 'Encyclopaedias to be precise.' He laughed unattractively. Two of his top teeth were very pointy.

'Oh?' I noticed there were a few missing, so I deduced they were in the holdall Emily had seen Jamie leave with. Why had he come back, though? Had he suddenly remembered he owed Toby?

'I can see you're wondering why Hugh, living in a hut in the middle of nowhere, would have a desperate need for encyclopaedias.'

I had a think. 'Was it to learn the world flags?'

'Nope.'

'To burn them to keep warm?'

'Nah, he'd never have done that.' Jamie put his spliff in a decorative bowl on the coffee table and got up. 'Come on, I'll show you.'

Worried he was about to take me to a cellar, I was relieved when he opened the front door and strode towards his car, parked half up on the pavement. He clunked it open and lifted the boot. By the time I caught up, he'd pulled a huge book out and laid it on top of coats and shoes.

'Open it at any page,' he told me.

'OK.' I did as I was told, and after turning a chunk of pages, there before us was a fifty-pound note.

'And again.'

This time I found a twenty and then a ten, then another twenty, then another fifty. 'Is it full of these?' I asked.

'Two of the books are. The third is a quarter full.'

Back in the house, he topped up our glasses in the kitchen. It was a cold, black, grey and metal room with some nice touches. A gorgeous pink vase full of unusual flowers. Brightly coloured tea towels. Two dainty cups and saucers with a pretty Chinese pattern on, plus a matching bowl. It was like a man designed the kitchen and a woman was trying to pretty it up.

Once settled in the living room, Jamie stared into his drink. I couldn't manage any more wine, not without a crisp or nut. Oh God, food. I checked the time and swore, then texted Billy. "So sorry, but caught up in work. Can we move to tomorrow? Edie xx"

'Hugh once told me, like ages ago, that he was squirrelling away… his exact words, off his head one night. Yeah, told me he was squirrelling away cash. Her cash. Loads of it. She leaves it lying around, he said. Always too much, for like trips out, and the twins, and paying music teachers, the cleaner and gardeners, and for Hugh or her mum to buy food… and workmen who only want cash. I tell you, Hugh reeled off this long, long list and said how fucking blind she was when it came to that kind of dough – like it was just play money, not part of her important business. Anyway… I said, oh yeah, where are you keeping that then? and he did this.' Jamie tapped the side of his nose, then knocked back more wine, put the glass down, picked up his joint and relit it.

After the silence that followed, I said, 'So he did tell you where, obviously.'

'Yep. But not till much later, after he'd run away. Flagged me down one day as I was leaving Fellford. Fucking scared the shit out of me, jumping from the bushes like that. I dropped him back by the woods. Said he'd walk from there, but never told me where to. We arranged to meet at that same spot in three days' time, and I was supposed to have the books with me.'

'But you didn't go?'

'No, I didn't. Couldn't work out how to get into the flat, then Jessica was staying there the next day. I feel fucking bad now. I'd given him twenty quid, but that wad he'd been squirrelling away might have saved his life.'

'You don't know that.'

He looked up from his glass. 'You're very nice.'

I smiled and he did his pointy-tooth smile back. 'OK if I make a cup of tea?' I asked.

'Of course,' he said, like it was his place. He wanted one too. 'Better sober up if I'm going to drive. In fact, make it a coffee. Please.'

I found teabags and the remains of some milk that smelt OK. There was one of those coffee machines, but since I'd never used one, I hunted through Jessica's cupboards for instant. Perhaps, like Astrid, she'd barred it from her house. But no, there it was, right at the back of a shelf I couldn't reach. At this point, I could have called for Jamie, but instead I hoicked myself up onto the counter and clung to the cupboard door handle.

'Yes!' I said, grabbing the jar.

But as I lowered one leg, the door swung outwards, and the jar of coffee slipped from my hand and fell on the counter. Soon after, I heard a smashing sound, then once back on solid ground I saw the Chinese-patterned bowl scattered over the floor. It was the one that matched the teacups. "Jasper" and "Conran", I read on two broken pieces. "Chinoiserie" said another.

'Everything OK?' shouted Jamie.

'Fine!' I called back while my head was swearing and panicking. It was bad enough to be trespassing, but destroying the owner's possibly valuable items? Shit, what to do, what to do…

The bowl was in too many pieces to be repaired, so all I could think of was hiding it. I found a dustpan and brush under the sink, swept up the china and tried the back door. Locked and no sign of a key.

Try the front, then you can go down the side passage to the back garden and maybe bury the evidence.

Good idea, I told whoever sent me that message.

I walked down the hall and past the open living room door. 'Just need to bin something!' I called out to Jamie, but he appeared to be asleep or in a trance.

Once in the back garden and about to open a bin, I spotted a wooden-framed area beside the small shed. I went over and, as I'd hoped, behind it was a compost bin. Hoping a rat wouldn't leap out and bite my throat, I bravely opened the lid, then stuck a hand in the contents and created a well. Into the well I dropped the crockery pieces, covering them with what looked like recently arrived cabbage leaves, potato peelings and carrot shavings. Jessica may have been in deep mourning, but she'd found time to produce proper meals for herself. Admirable.

Back in the flat, Jamie was still asleep. I went through a lobby off the kitchen and into a bathroom where I washed all the gunk off my hands with some great-smelling liquid soap, dried them, and stared at the tempting glass-fronted cabinet hanging on the wall. Just a quick look wouldn't hurt. Inside were three things: tampons, pink lady razors and a box of medication. The label said to take one or two at night. Sleeping tablets, I guessed. Poor Jessica, I thought, as though suddenly realising what a horrible time she'd been through.

I put the medication back in the cabinet, wiped fingerprints off the glass door, then gave the kitchen a final clean up before starting the whole coffee business again.

* * *

'The obvious question is,' I said to freshly caffeinated Jamie. 'Why are you picking up Hugh's money now? Or rather, Jessica's money.' There was his pressing debt with Toby, of course.

'Ah. Right.' He wriggled in his chair and leaned forward. 'OK, you're not going to like or approve of this, but…'

'Yes?'

'I wanted to give it to my sister. Zara got into some debt – like a lot – helping out Hugh.'

'So you think she deserves it more than rich Jessica?'

'With a fucking great house in Primrose Hill? Too right I think Zara deserves it. Plus, Hugh had promised her they'd be so well off once he was divorced. And that's all gone now. So, yeah.'

'But it's theft, Jamie.'

'Doesn't feel like it.'

'I know, but really, you should give it to Jessica. Or put the books back on the shelves, at least.'

He stared at me for a while, and I became uncomfortable.

'Yeah, you're right, dammit.' He got up slowly and headed out to his car. I fully expected him to rev up and drive off, but he came back in with the bag and put the books back. Whether he'd quickly removed some of those notes, I'd never know.

TWELVE

So, here I was in Billy's kitchen, having stayed overnight after a late-evening dash to his. It was rather lovely, this home he'd ploughed his hard-earned City bonuses into. It was in the middle of Elmbridge, a village five miles to the west of Oxford, and not that far from places I'd recently visited for the Jessica case.

I wandered, not room to room, as most internal walls had been removed, but area to area... kitchen, living, dining, office. The house had been built in the sixteen hundreds and its outside walls were as thick as tree trunks. I sat on one of the window seats, created by those walls, cradling my tea and watching Elmbridgers go about their business for a while.

Billy was currently slicing the sourdough bread he'd made, having explained how he kept his culture alive by regularly adding flour and water, and how he often gave bits of the culture to his neighbour, Naomi, and vice versa.

'Fancy a walk after breakfast?' he asked. 'I'll give you a tour of the metropolis that is Elmbridge.'

'Don't you have to go to work?'

'I sometimes work from home, and Georgia more or less runs the place, so, no. One egg or two?'

'One, please.'

'OK, tomato and one egg on sourdough toast coming up.'

'I need to see Astrid later,' I told him. 'At two.'

She'd texted me first thing, sounding uncharacteristically keen to meet up. I'd see her instead of Mike and Emily, so I messaged them both asking to move our meeting forward a day.

'Do you have to?' asked Billy.

'I'd like to. It would feel like a bit of normality.'

Billy twirled his spatula around. 'And this doesn't?'

I got up, put my tea on a chunky white side table – the décor was a mix of modern, antique, and ethnic – and went and cuddled him from behind. 'A gorgeous man cooking for me in his very nice home is definitely not normal.'

'It could become the new normal?'

'Fat chance,' I said. 'I'm just not that lucky.'

Billy put his implement down and gave me a proper hug. 'Stay here with me?' he asked. 'While your house is being done.'

'But I've only known you five minutes. And don't you mean you and Noah?'

'Ah yeah, forgot about him. Mind you, there's a newish girlfriend. He's often at her place. She's very sweet, and it seems serious. Her parents breed horses.'

'And what does she do?'

'Apart from having very loud sex with my son? A lot of Instagramming, apparently. She's good for Noah, so I'm hoping she'll be a keeper.' He scooped up an egg and placed it on a slice of toast. 'Noah's been through a few girlfriends, though. Too handsome for his own good. OK, grub's up. You sit there, so you have a view of the birds.'

'Thank you.' I took my seat. Beyond the half-open French doors were assorted birds swooping, landing, and taking off again. 'Did you throw food out there especially for my benefit?'

'Of course not!' He placed a great-looking breakfast in front of me and kissed the top of my head. 'I got Noah to do it especially for your benefit.'

* * *

Elmbridge was just the right side of twee to be liveable. There was a village square, rather than a green, and a mix of house styles from ancient and thatched, like Billy's, to Victorian, to thirties, to fifties council housing, to modern. I'd never seen a village with so many shops, and the place was buzzing. According to Billy, the only essentials you couldn't pick up in Elmbridge were Thai food and new shoes.

We'd ended up at a table outside a pub in the square. It was feeling autumnal so I had a hot chocolate. There was a pretty church beside us and an art exhibition in what Billy told me used to be a tiny school, right in the middle of the square. From where we sat, I could see a deli, another pub, an estate agent, and the Co-op.

'It's the excellent secondary school that keeps the village alive,' Billy said. 'Just wish Noah had taken advantage of its excellence when he was there.'

'I'm sure he'll be fine. He'll marry this new girlfriend and take over her family's breeding business. You'll be relieved he didn't ace his A-levels and end up in lower-middle management for decades.'

'I dunno. I'm pretty sure he's terrified of horses.'

'Oh.' I laughed, then yet another woman between the ages of thirty and fifty called out, 'Hi, Ben!' in far too flirty a manner.

To be fair, a similar number of males had greeted him, or he them. What was this oddly cheerful and communicative Truman Show-like place?

'It's spookily friendly,' I whispered.

He grinned and waved at a distant mother and child. 'On the surface, yeah.'

'Are you saying Elmbridge is a steaming cauldron of gossip, backstabbing and infidelity?'

'Well, they don't call it Ambridge for nothing. Luckily, none of it impinges on my life.'

'Don't speak too soon,' I said after a middling attractive woman beamed at Billy, looked at me, and got straight on her phone.

* * *

With no time to pop home and check out the kitchen, I went straight to Astrid's.

'Shoes off,' she said, staring at my feet.

'Sorry, just walked around a field.' I took them off and followed her through the kitchen and across her neat lawn to the shed. When she began rolling a spliff, I said, 'Not for me.'

'Well, that's a first,' she said, shaking her head in disbelief. 'Must be this Billy. Honestly, Edie, no sooner do you get a man than you're absorbing all his habits, interests, morals and preferences.'

Was that true?

'Do you remember Keith?' she went on. 'Three, four years ago? Got you drinking pints of real ale and morris dancing.'

'Not at the same time.'

'In, where was it again… Little Boring?'

'Great Goring. And it was fun. I enjoyed it. Both.' Keith had collected beer mats, but then pubs stopped providing them. On one date he'd gone through all four hundred for me. He was very easy on the eye, though.

'Like Keanu Reeves with bells and tassels,' someone had said.

'The only guy you didn't do that with,' said Astrid, 'was–'

'Greg?'

'Yes. Before my time, but you have talked endlessly about him.'

'That's true. And you're right, I definitely did my own thing with him. I don't remember him having any hobbies, though.'

'There was the one,' said Astrid, cocking her head. 'But if you'd taken up that, you'd have been screwing young women, one after the other, after the other–'

'OK, OK,' I snapped. 'There were only a couple, maybe three. Anyway, why did you want to see me today?'

'To have a catch-up. I read about Hugh in *The Oxford Times* and wondered how the case was going.'

'How long have you got?' I asked, calming down.

She picked up her phone. 'Twenty-seven minutes.'

'Right…' I said, and gave her a summary of what had happened, including the Toby business and the Jamie encounter.

'My, you have been busy,' she said. She looked around with glazed eyes and the odd facial twitch. Were the wheels and cogs doing their work and, when ready, would she come out with something useful? Something insightful, or wise?

I sat waiting, trying not to stare at her by taking in the un-fired pots, the tubs of glass and stone mosaic bits, and the upright tube of glue.

'Left- or right-opening fridge?' she asked.

'Sorry?'

'Your new fridge-freezer. It'll be inside a unit, obviously, and positioned…' She found pen and paper and drew a rough plan. 'Here. The cooker will be to the left of it, and the sink to the right. So, which would be most ergonomically useful? Left opening, or right opening?'

I closed my eyes. 'OK, so... right opening? Or do I mean left?' I drew a handle on the plan.

'Yes, I'd have gone for that. They tend to be reversible these days, but still. Oh, Lord, is that the time? I need to pick up anchovies on the way to school. Last time I shopped with Jakob after pick up, he had a meltdown over some rip-off magazine with a free laser gun.'

'You don't like him having guns?'

'I don't mind at all. It just wasn't on our shopping list. And he knew it.'

'Maybe that was a bit...' I stopped myself. Crossing the lawn, I asked when she thought the kitchen would be finished.

'A week Friday,' she said, perfectly straight-faced.

I laughed. 'Really?'

'Drop by at four-thirty?'

'It's a date!' I told her.

In the house, she got together her bag, phone, and an after-school snack for Jakob.

Once out front, where I admired her neatly pruned Ceanothus, Astrid said, 'Has anyone checked if there are any magic mushrooms near those woods?'

'I'm not sure.'

'And this Toby.'

'Yes?'

'Could he get hold of death cap mushrooms?'

'Who knows?' I said as she strode off.

'Emily?' she called out from a distance.

THIRTEEN

'So, Ben paid Toby a visit in prison,' said Emily.

'And?' I asked, perking up. I'd passed on Astrid's question but made out it was mine. I'd also told Mike and

Emily about finding the keys to Toby's flat and everything that happened after, including spotting what might have been a painting Hugh had stolen from Jessica. Emily had, it turned out, been doing yoga nearby and had locked her bike outside his place.

'He swore he'd never ordered death cap mushrooms for anyone. In fact, he swore he'd never sold any drugs to anyone. Apparently, he'd never seen that painting in his flat either. Said someone must have planted it. I'm worried now that some clever lawyer will get him off. Ben keeps telling me that's not going to happen cos they've got statements from other people, including some neighbour who's heard and seen stuff. Underage girls included.'

'Presumably,' I said, 'the police found evidence in his flat?'

'They did, yeah. I shouldn't fret so much.'

Mike chewed on his pen. 'I still think our theory is correct and Toby got the death cap for someone.'

'Maybe his mashed-up brain can't remember,' said Emily. 'Or chooses not to, cos he wouldn't want to be, like, implicated in murder. All I know is, when I lived there, Toby was asked to get hold of all sorts of weird shit. Frog venom, peyote, nutmeg. Sometimes at really short notice. So, yeah, maybe you're right?'

'Can't you go to Tesco for nutmeg?' I said. I was sure I had some in a cupboard. No cupboards, I remembered.

'It's raw nutmeg that gets you high. The stuff in shops is roasted and, like, the magic ingredient gets killed off. I'm not sure, but I might've tried it. Anyway, for the right price, I reckon Toby would know someone, who might know someone, who could lay their hands on deadly shrooms.'

'Toby may have played a role,' Mike said, 'but if no one can prove he did order it, and who for, then the real culprit might never be known. It could be anyone.'

'Even Hugh at a stretch,' I said. 'Say he was planning on using it on his wife, but accidentally poisoned himself?'

Mike nodded. 'That's not a bad theory. Jessica did say Hugh was careless. And then there's Zara. She and Hugh did have a row, remember?' He got up and slung his bag over himself. 'Anyone up for a Cat Burger? I've learned that I have to eat before teaching. Don't want to lose it over an unhyphenated compound adjective again.'

Emily got her phone out. 'Can't, sorry,' she said tapping away.

'I'll come along and have a coffee,' I told Mike. 'I can't eat much these days.'

'Love?' he asked.

'No, no. More like my house.'

'Aw,' said Emily. 'That's a shame.'

FOURTEEN

The following Friday, at half four on the dot, I knocked on my slightly ajar front door, my other hand anxiously squeezing Billy's.

'Yoo hoo!' I called out to no response. I let go of Billy and he followed me down the short bit of hallway still remaining and into the large knocked-through-and-extended living-sitting-kitchen area.

Across the middle of the room hung three of Gary's plastic sheets, and my combined high spirits and nervousness became plain nervousness. Why was the back of the room blocked off?

'Damn,' I said. 'It isn't finished after all.'

Why hadn't Astrid told me?

'Ah well, never mind,' said Billy. 'Feeling brave enough to look behind the plastic?'

'I'm not sure.'

After walking over the new and very lovely pale-oak floor of the living area, I took a deep breath and gingerly pulled back the screen.

A loud chorus of, 'SURPRISE!!' rang out from not only Astrid and Gary, but Mike and Emily, Gary's lads, and even, to my astonishment, Jessica.

Astrid put a glass in my hand while Mike opened a bottle of champagne. I looked around my completely stunning, pale and shiny, and matt and sleek, and here and there steel, kitchen. My mouth opened, but I was unable to utter anything.

'It's even nicer than mine!' called out Jessica. 'I'm jealous!'

Everyone laughed and bubbly was poured and a toast to the new kitchen, and to Astrid and Gary, was made by Mike.

'It's beautiful,' I told Astrid. I was tearful and she let me hug her for once. 'Thank you so much.'

'I've got the perfect table for you, arriving tomorrow, along with six bucket seats in a mix of colours.'

'Wow,' I kept saying, as she took me on a tour, opening doors to cupboards with racks in, recycling units in, a dishwasher. A dishwasher! And an island! With stylish bar stools! I ran my hands over smooth surfaces, inspected the huge fridge-freezer, and took in the light pouring through the four overhead Velux windows. It was so lovely, it was scary. All this for me?

'When's the dinner party then, Edie?' asked Gary. 'I'll put it in my diary!'

'You do all know I can't cook for toffee, right?'

Everyone laughed and my glass was filled by Mike. I held it up towards Jessica. 'Although I know a woman who can!'

She smiled and lifted her glass. 'It'd be my pleasure.'

When Billy sidled up beside me, I said, 'Were you in on it?'

'Of course.' He grinned and kissed my cheek. 'This may all be wasted on you, but congratulations.'

'You'll be using it too, I hope?'

'As long as you clear up afterwards? You do it so well.'

'I do.' Now I'd learned how. Billy had a cutlery system. All spoons had to spoon. Mugs were arranged with the tallest at the back, handles facing forwards. I was still trying to get the hang of his dishwasher rules.

Emily held a plate of sausage rolls in front of us. 'Don't worry, they're veggie. They are, aren't they, Billy?'

'Did you make them?' I asked.

'Yep. They're vegan, in fact. I've finally taken that step.'

A hundred per cent vegan? I wanted to cry, but I couldn't, not on such a happy occasion. I popped one of his dinky rolls in my mouth, went, 'Mmm,' and slipped my arm around him.

'Gorgeous,' he said.

'Thank you.'

'I meant the kitchen.'

'Ha ha.'

I put my head on his shoulder and found myself wondering what Greg would have made of my new home. If I'd had an island back then, would he still have left in the middle of our living-together experiment?

Someone called out that we needed photos, so I let go of Billy and high-fived Astrid for the cameras.

'No putting them on social media!' I said.

I took some photos too, then sent them to Maeve. When she FaceTimed me a couple of minutes later, she had tears pouring down her cheeks. 'I can't believe that's my home,' she sobbed. 'The one I grew up in? Really?'

'Really,' I told her. Was she gutted? Memories of my terrible meals, Alfie in his highchair, the chaos.

'It's fucking brilliant,' she said, trying to laugh and cry at the same time.

'Mummy swored!' said Alfie, looming into view.

'Sorry, Alfie,' said Maeve. 'You like Gran's new kitchen too, don't you?'

I braced myself for a poo comment, frantically turning down the volume, as Jessica and Mike were beside me talking property.

'It's like a SPACESHIP!' he said before disappearing.

'I'll take that,' I told Maeve, and said I'd call her back later for a proper chat.

When Mike went off to put the brand-new kettle on, I thanked Jessica for coming and asked how she and the boys were doing.

'We're OK, I think. They've released… the body. And we've got a date for the funeral now, so lots to organise and keep my mind off things. The boys have gone back to school and seem happier for it.'

'That's good.'

'Sorry, I feel like a bit of a gate crasher. I bumped into Emily yesterday and she invited me. More the merrier, she said. I, er, also saw Zara yesterday. It was my reason for coming to Oxford. I just felt we should talk, since we'll both be at the funeral.'

I might have been a bit more startled by this if I hadn't just endured a surprise party. 'How did it go?'

'It was a little awkward. I'm not sure how real she is, to be honest. Or perhaps she's shy. She and I may be performers in our catering personas, but I sensed that, like me, she's quite reserved. Hugh must have a type… had a type. Although we're physically different, at least facially. Anyway, I'm glad we did it, but, well, let's just say we're never going to be best friends.'

'That's understandable,' I said. 'I guess there aren't any developments that we've not heard about?'

'Not that I know of.'

'So, since they've found no evidence of foul play amongst family and friends, it does look as though Hugh came across some dodgy mushrooms… somewhere, somehow. Or was given them.'

'By a person unknown,' said Jessica.

'And likely to remain that way,' I said. 'The police have been pretty thorough so far, according to Ben. DS Watson. But, you know, police resources are limited, and new cases come along...'

'It's just so tragic. He may have had a wandering eye... actually, scratch that. A wandering dick' – her face suddenly looked pained – 'but he always came back to us. And he would have done again. He loved the boys... and I know he still had feelings for me, no matter what Zara or anyone else thinks. I wouldn't have divorced him, not really. It was just a way to get his attention. Get him back. Deep down, that was probably why I came to you guys.' Jessica's nose reddened and her eyes welled up. She grabbed a serviette. 'Sorry, sorry. You know, it's almost harder to accept now than at first. I just suddenly really miss the bastard, that's the problem.'

I was obviously in a huggy mood, as I gave her one too. When we pulled apart, I said, 'Going back to the mushrooms. Do you know if Hugh knew Toby Cargill? He lives almost directly over the road from you in Divinity Road.'

'The police asked me that.' She frowned and wiped her nose again. 'I told them I didn't and asked who he was. But they wouldn't say.'

'Toby's a drug dealer. I know someone who knows him.'

'Oh, right. Do you think Hugh bought the magic mushrooms from this Toby, and that maybe there was a rogue poisonous one in with them? Did the police interview him?'

'They did. He claimed not to know anything about any drugs. He's currently on remand for dealing and other offences, so has clammed up.'

'Bit of a dead end, then? Oh dear, wrong word...' She welled up again. 'I wonder if we'll ever know, or if the coroner will declare it death by misadventure, or some such phrase, and that'll be it?'

'You OK, Jessica?' asked Emily. 'Thanks for the champers, really tasty and nice tiny bubbles. Look, I took this amazing photo of you.'

Emily gestured for me to go and circulate while Jessica went, 'Ooh, yes, do forward me that one.'

I couldn't find Gary, then discovered him loading up his van. 'Thank you,' I said. 'I love the kitchen, and, well, all of it. And thanks also' – I lowered my voice – 'for working so well with Astrid. She's not everyone's cup of tea.'

'Hard to believe,' he said, hoisting a heavy toolbox onto the passenger seat, 'but then I have lived with Cruella de Vil for forty years.' He gave me a wink. 'We should be done painting upstairs in a week or two, then the house is all yours.'

'Ah, brilliant. Can't wait.'

Gary stopped, rubbed his head, and looked directly at me. 'Why not have a bit of a holiday with that chappie of yours while we're finishing off? It's term time, so you might find a bargain. I can recommend the Seychelles. Beautiful. Although Stella preferred Vietnam. Bhutan, now there's a fascinating place to explore. Trekked and camped, we did. Take my advice, though, Edie. Do it before your knees go.'

'I will,' I promised.

Before climbing in his van, even Gary got a hug.

FIFTEEN

It rained for two days straight in Lyme Regis – Billy's idea for a getaway. We played minigolf several times, our hoods up, our wet jeans sticking to our legs. We had endless cups of teas and coffees in various establishments, switching to alcohol at six. We worked through a book of crosswords – my idea – and had a meal out both evenings – vegan or veggie, of course, because Billy really had taken the plunge and I couldn't bring myself to eat dead animal in front of him.

Then on the third day, when it chucked it down again, we loaded up Billy's car and headed to London, where it continued to rain but at least we had museums and art galleries to while away the time in. We went up the Shard, but for post-Terence-trauma reasons, I declined a spin on the Eye. I promised Billy I'd tell him the whole Terence story one day, then an hour later poured it all out to him over two surprisingly tasty plant-based pizzas and a bottle of white.

Billy wiped away my tears, and holding my hand, stared at me with those penetrative brown eyes. 'You've been through so much.'

'I have. Maeve too. But we're fine now. Honestly.'

His look turned quizzical. 'I think you're strong, but I don't think you're as strong as you think.'

'There were a lot of "thinks" in that sentence,' I said. 'More wine?'

'Actually, I might have had enough.'

'Oh, go on.'

'I'm good.' Billy cupped my hand again. 'You do know that dating me involves a good degree of tedium?'

'Of course! I mean, no it doesn't. And even if it does, I like it. Shit.'

He laughed. 'I've been thinking…'

'What have you been thinking, Billy?'

'That we could work something out. Have a schedule?'

'It doesn't sound very romantic.'

'Going home to our separate houses might be less romantic?'

He had a point. 'OK, then. Maybe you could do a, what's it called… spreadsheet?' I chortled and knocked back more wine.

Billy smiled at me.

'What?' I asked again.

'Have you even seen one?'

'Not really.'

He gently pulled his hand from mine and picked up his water. 'How about a week at yours together, a week at mine together, then a week in our separate places?'

'What if I want to visit Maeve and family?'

'You could do that in your week off from me, or we'd both go during together weeks?'

I closed one eye so I could see him better. 'You've been thinking about this, haven't you?'

'I have. Haven't you?'

I shook my head. 'Not much of a planner.'

'This I've noticed.'

'What do you mean?'

He ate some of the pizza while he thought about it. 'You know, you can tell a lot about a person by the way they pack?'

'Like a suitcase?'

'Yeah, or a car. A planner will know what to take because they know more or less exactly what they'll be doing, wherever they're going.'

'Are you making this up?'

'Yes, but stay with me. When you pack, say for a long-weekend trip to Brighton, what do you take?'

'Way too much, usually.'

'Why?'

'To cover all eventualities, I suppose.'

'My point exactly. Not a planner.'

I didn't get it. Surely that was still planning? I decided not to pursue the conversation and just stared at his nice eyes, while I got drunker and he got soberer.

We walked under one umbrella back towards London Bridge, stopping by the Tate Modern entrance for shelter. I looked up at my dad – or rather, at the swirling rain in the lamplight. Am I doing the right thing? I asked. Send me a sign if I am.

'Right,' said Billy, after several minutes of nothing happening. No thunder rumble, no lightening crack. He hooked his arm through mine. 'Hot chocolate in our room?'

I checked the time on my phone: 7.52.

SIXTEEN

I'd pictured a small gathering of friends and family at my New Year's Eve party – something not much bigger than my surprise kitchen reveal. But there I was, answering the door to guest number forty- or fifty-something: a woman I'd chatted to occasionally in the last century when our tiny kids were briefly friends, and whose name I couldn't recall. I'd bumped into a few days back and rashly invited her. She'd brought her daughter Sophia.

'Come in, come in,' I said. 'Gosh, Sophia, look at you! Help yourselves to a drink.'

I left them and found Maeve and her growing bump – due mid-April. She had the pregnancy glow, now she was over the sickness, and her dark and curly one-quarter-Spanish hair was thicker and shinier than ever.

'What's Sophia's mum's name?' I asked. 'Do you remember?'

'Not really. Oh, wow, there's Sophia!' Maeve disappeared and left Jack tugging something from Alfie's hand.

'No more breadsticks,' he told Alfie. 'Try some of Gran's quiche… No, it's not poo, it's delicious.'

'Don't they ever grow out of that?' I asked.

It was actually Billy's quiche. Vegan. Jack cut a slice, put it in a bowl and handed it to Alfie with a spoon. 'Listen, Alf, if you stop saying poo for the rest of the party, I'll give you twenty pounds and you can spend it in town tomorrow. What do you say?'

Alfie frowned and said, 'OK,' before leaving his quiche on the table and running off.

Jack turned to me. 'Don't tell Maeve. She's not keen on bribery as a parenting tool.'

'I won't. So… have you come up with a name for the baby yet?'

'No, well, yes. But we're not telling anyone because you know how that goes. People can't help but express their horror. "I had an evil aunt called Doreen!"'

'I take it it's not Doreen?'

'It isn't.' He waved at Mike across the room. 'This is great, Edie, but we'll need to head off soon. Get back to Brighton by Maeve's bedtime. She's asleep before Alfie most nights.'

'Ah, poor thing.'

'You mean me, I hope? A full day in the café, then a full evening cooking, chasing my son around, cleaning the house.'

'Any prospective nannies?'

'Nope. I'm beginning to think they've all heard about Alfie. We'll definitely need help after April, especially as Maeve's threatening to put in hours at the café once she can fit behind the counter again.'

'Oh dear. Well I've told her I'm happy to help out. For the first couple of weeks, that is. I do have Billy to think about now.'

'Yeah, you don't want to lose that one. How's it going?'

'Pretty well,' I said. 'We've got this schedule. One week we live here, one week we live at his, and the third week we go our own ways.'

'God, that sounds so civilised.'

'It does, doesn't it? Only… I don't know, perhaps I'm not cut out for schedules.'

'Maybe it'll be good for you? I mean, it's great when you phone out of the blue to say you're on your way down to us, but…'

'I know Maeve sometimes gets thrown by it.' I laughed. 'She's always been more organised than me. Less…'

'Spontaneous?'

'That's the word.'

'I take it Billy isn't?'

'Well…' Perhaps I shouldn't share our, no *his*, Saturday – and if we have the time and energy, Wednesday – intimacy schedule with my daughter's partner. 'Billy finds routine comforting.'

We both looked over at him.

'Really nice guy,' Jack said.

'He is.'

Billy was talking to the Headington lot, Mike, Seth, and Zara. Nice Buns was Mike's local eatery now he'd bought a flat nearby. He'd even had Zara and her new partner over for dinner. Billy and I had gone too, and I'd hit it off with Zara, who turned out to be mildly outrageous when not politely running her café. She and I had met up for a pre-Christmas drink, which turned into four, and she told me tales of her travels, and about her parents selling up the business because neither she nor Jamie wanted to take it over.

It was nice getting everyone together. Old colleagues from my teaching days. Neighbours, including a couple who'd complained endlessly about noise and illegal parking when my house was being done up. Now they were saying they might do the same to their place. 'Revenge?' I'd asked them. 'Ha, ha.'

Gary and Stella were hitting it off with Emily's parents, and appeared to be trying to set up some music. I went to see if I could help.

'It's this Bluetooth lark,' said Gary. 'Can't get my playlist to come out the blooming speakers.'

'Here.' I took his phone and went into settings, for once feeling more practical than my builder. When, to my surprise and delight, Bronski Beat blasted out, I adjusted the volume, bowed, and put the phone on my gorgeous off-white quartz stone counter.

A small table near the front door was now covered in, and surrounded by, housewarming presents I hadn't been expecting – ranging from a bunch of supermarket flowers to Astrid's fantastic concrete wall clock with bright orange hands. She'd told me exactly where to hang it, of course.

Jessica had also turned up with her sons and two cushions, which I hoped would grow on me – the cushions, not the boys. It turned out the twins had chosen them, which made me like them even more – the cushions and the boys. She'd also brought along Christine, her mother. Christine was unlike her daughter in every way – five foot, blonde and curvy. She'd given me a firm hug and said, 'Lovely to meet you at last,' with northern vowels, and I'd instantly taken to her.

The boys were upstairs now with other teens, and while her gregarious mother mixed, Jessica reorganised the food table. She'd either slipped into professional-caterer mode, or, as she'd once told me, she was quite shy. A bit of both? She was spending much more time in Oxford now, having rented the flat above hers on Divinity Road and made it the boys' pad. The Primrose Hill house was about to be let, so she wasn't completely burning bridges.

She and I had been out a few times, mainly for lunches but once to another Off Beats gig, where she'd danced for an hour then cried on my shoulder in the ladies because she missed dancing with Hugh.

That hadn't been long after the funeral, and she'd grown stronger since then, throwing herself back into her business and 'masses of yoga'.

The doorbell rang, so I went to see who it was and if I remembered their name.

I did. It was Emily.

'Finally!' I said.

She stepped in and prised off her boots, then dug into her large bag and handed me an unwrapped gift. "The How to Cook, Cookbook", it said on the front. "For Men".

'I couldn't find one for women,' she said. 'That's why I'm late. I expect they just think all women can–'

'Very thoughtful, Emily. Thank you.'

She pulled another present from her bag. 'Don't worry, we did get you something else. It's a late Christmas present, from me and Ben.'

'Ooh,' I said. 'Can I open it now?'

'Course.'

I undid the pretty pink bow, took off the paper and lifted the lid of a neat white box to discover a phone that looked exactly like the one I already had.

'Oh,' I said.

'I know what you're thinking,' she said. 'I chose the same size as yours cos I know you hate the big one you bought me.'

'Hate is a bit strong.'

'But this one is, like, the latest, and it takes brilliant pictures and is quick, but best of all, the battery lasts for ages. You know how you drive us all nuts with your phone running out of charge.'

'That's brilliant, Em. And so generous. Too generous! But thank you. You don't know how happy this will make Billy. And me, of course.' I led her to the drinks table, where I pointed out the soft fruit punch.

'I do love your house, Edie,' said Jessica's mum, suddenly beside me.

'Thanks, Christine. My builder did a fantastic job, with a bit of help from Astrid.' I pointed her out.

'We met.' She chuckled while she filled her glass with white wine. 'She asked if I'd considered intermittent fasting.'

'Oh, Lord.' I told Christine some of the insults Astrid had lobbed my way, such as, 'You know, it wouldn't cost a fortune to get those upper-eye bags removed.'

Christine and I fell about.

'I hadn't even known I had them!' I said. 'Now they're the first things I see in the mirror.'

'You've got a good face,' Christine said, scanning it. 'Leave it natural, yeah?'

'Don't worry, I was planning to.'

Christine looked over at her daughter stacking dirty plates on a tray. 'I wish Jessica had left hers alone, but I suppose when you marry a chap seventeen years younger, the fillers and knife jobs must be tempting.'

'She looks great, I have to say.'

Christine's expression changed. She took a good glug of wine, and then another. 'It was wasted on him, though. All her efforts to stay youthful.'

'Mm,' I said, not wanting to agree or disagree.

'Don't get me wrong, I liked Hugh, at least to begin with. Good-looking, charming, great with the boys and full of compliments for his mother-in-law. The life and soul of any party. What was not to like?'

'Obviously, I never met him.'

'No. But anyway, when Jessica told me what he'd done...'

'Being cheated on is horrible,' I said. 'Believe me, I know.'

'Not the other women, no. Although that was bad enough. I mean... Actually, maybe we shouldn't... not here.'

'Oh?' Now I needed a drink. I found a glass, filled it with wine and turned back to Christine. I produced a warm smile and gently nudged her. 'No one can hear us. Go on.'

She dipped her head and slowly shook it from side to side, staring into her empty glass. 'She told you about her accident, did she?'

'On her bike? Yes.'

'But not the whole story, I'd imagine. Not what actually went down, and who was…'

'Who was what?'

'Emily, don't drink that fruit punch!' yelled Alfie, charging at the table and bashing into me. 'It tastes like wee!'

'Alfie!' I said sternly. 'Remember your promise to Jack?'

'But I didn't say poo!'

'Ha, ha, you just said it!' I bent down and tickled him and promised I wouldn't tell.

When I turned to Christine, she was chatting to my formerly angry neighbours.

Damn. I'd have to catch her again later.

At some point, after we'd seen in the new year, the music volume went right up, and in the area that used to be my front room, Astrid was dancing with Jessica's boys. Others joined them.

I went and had a quick vodka shot for dance courage, and then another. Before I knew it, I was partnered with a father I'd fancied in the playground twenty-odd years ago. What was his name? He was still attractive, but danced in an alarming way, like he was receiving a series of electric shocks. I decided to name him Buzz and laughed at my brilliant joke. Or maybe at his dancing…

Billy was watching us, and I gave him a wave. Had I spoken to him at all, I wondered, and thought perhaps I hadn't. He looked good. Very Billy Bob Thornton.

I sent Buzz off to fetch me a drink and when Billy didn't want to join me for a dance, saying 'You really should drink some water, Edie,' I said, 'Fuck water,' and went and danced alongside Astrid and the boys.

When the music went off at one in the morning and guests began to leave, I wondered where Christine was. I knew I needed to talk to her, but couldn't quite remember why.

SEVENTEEN

The next morning, Billy rose early, saying he had to go and catch up on some pre-Christmas orders and that he'd go back to his place tonight to clear up after Noah.

'We are actually due to have our week apart from today,' he said on his way out. 'No point in disrupting the schedule.'

'God forbid,' I said back under the duvet, then smiled. I loved him dearly, but a whole week to myself!

I slept on until my headache almost disappeared, and around ten I had a leisurely breakfast. It was sunny out, so I did a little tour of the bare and wintery garden and thought about seeing what Astrid was up to. As I picked up my phone, a call came through from Zara.

'Hi, Edie,' she said. 'Happy New Year!'

'And to you!'

'I just wanted to thank you for the really nice party.'

'Ah, glad you enjoyed it. And thanks for the present.' It had been a voucher for an evening meal at Nice Buns. "To give Billy a break from the cooking!" she'd written, with a drawn laughing emoji, and I'd instantly regretted sharing that with her.

'You're welcome. So, what are you and Billy up to today?'

I told her he'd had to go into work and that I might at some point wander into the office. 'Or not,' I added. 'How about you?'

'I'm actually in Fellford making a start on my parents' packing. As I said, they've got a buyer for the house and business, and he wants things to happen soon.'

'That's good.'

'It is and it isn't. Mum and Dad had to move themselves to the coast after Christmas because Dad's breathing got much worse.'

'Oh, I'm sorry.'

'The sea air usually sorts him out. Anyway, Jamie's still fast asleep upstairs, as he got hammered at some party, and always-keen-to-help Lucy is at her parents... so, it's currently just me wrapping and packing and chucking. Mum and Dad can't house most of this stuff down in Bournemouth. So, anyway... I thought I'd take you up on your kind offer to come over and help today.'

'Um...' What kind offer? I thought Zara must be confusing me with someone else, but then the fog cleared a little and I recalled saying something vaguely along those lines, just as she was leaving and I wasn't feeling too good.

'Yes, yes,' I said. 'Of course!'

Shit.

'I thought you could have a poke around, too. Maybe there'll be one or two things you might like? For free?'

'Oh?' I said, a bit thrown. Did she think my house was underfurnished? Or was she in need of moral support? Maybe she was just being kind. 'Actually, I could do with large plant pots for the garden.'

Astrid had done a grand job with the small firs dotted here and there and the grey metal bench, but a minimalist garden can be a cold and unwelcoming garden.

'We've got pots galore,' said Zara. 'Out on the patio. Mum's taken her favourites but there are plenty left.'

'Well, if you're sure? Shall I come soon?'

'Please do!'

'Right. I'll need to shower, dry my hair... so see you in about—'

'Don't you need directions?'

Oops. She said she'd text me the address.

* * *

Just before two, I pulled up on the drive next to Jamie's black car. No sign of Zara's car, but perhaps it was around the back. I thought about my first visit here with Mike. I'd come across Lucy a couple of times since playing the part of Heather, but she'd shown no signs of recognition. Perhaps the bad accent and the dog had distracted her from my face.

Zara let me in, and after I dumped my bag and hung up my coat, she led me through to the kitchen and continued wrapping something in newspaper.

'This is all going to the charity shops,' she said. 'Listen, why don't you wander around and write down anything that takes your fancy? There's a pad and several pens over on the dresser. Oh, avoid the attic. It's where Jamie lives, and you won't find anything but socks and dirty plates there.'

'Got it.' I decided to start up in the bedrooms.

The first I entered was small. A single bed and a desk. Could I use a small wooden desk with a drawer? I'd paint it, perhaps, and have it in the third bedroom, previously Alfie's room. I flipped open the notepad and started a list.

Skipping the bathroom, I looked around a second bedroom and wrote "Anglepoise lamp?" Next came the master bedroom, which contained only Mrs Peacock's candlewick robe. In a small study off the landing were two white filing cabinets. I added them to my list for the Fox Wilder office.

'Edie?' croaked Jamie behind me.

I spun around. He wore only a short towel. His eyes were puffy, and water dripped down his face and onto his pale hairless chest.

'Hi, Jamie,' I said, quickly averting my gaze and picking up a large stapler. 'Zara told me to choose anything I might want, as your parents don't have room for everything.'

'Cool, yeah. Knock yourself out.' He turned to go, then stopped. 'I've bagsied the filing cabinets, by the way.'

'Ah.' I crossed them off my list and added the stapler.

Downstairs in the cloakroom, a blue and white soap dish caught my eye, as did a nest of glass tables in the living room. Billy and I were constantly balancing plates and mugs on the sofa arms, so he'd be pleased.

By the time I'd gone around a cold and formal dining room, where I took a shine to a blue glass vase and made my way back to the kitchen, Jamie was there, dressed and brewing coffee while making himself toast.

Zara rolled her eyes at me. 'Jamie,' she said, 'you don't fancy rustling up some lunch, do you?'

There was a pause before he said, 'Sure. What do you fancy?'

Zara put down a half-wrapped plate and inspected the contents of the fridge. 'You could occasionally shop, you know?'

Jamie sighed. 'I didn't think you'd be starting all this today, or I would have done. Anyway, Zar, there's still loads of Mum and Dad's frozen ready meals to get through.'

They both laughed.

'They're not known for their cooking skills, our parents,' Zara said. 'Not sure where Jamie and I got ours from.' She yanked open the freezer and pulled out a drawer. 'Family-size chicken casserole?' She handed him a large box. 'There might be some frozen green beans or peas.' Zara turned my way. 'You OK with all this, Edie?'

'Yes, sounds great.' I was just being polite, what with my late breakfast. 'I'll go and check out the garden while it's heating up.'

'The shed's full of stuff too!' she called out as I walked through a lobby, past a utility room and into the second living area. It was more like a conservatory, or sunroom.

I slid open the glass doors, then stepped onto the paving stones of the raised patio. What a gorgeous garden, I thought, even in January. Lots of mature trees and shrubs. Unfortunately, not even the tallest of trees could hide the backdrop – a huge storage block shouting "PEACOCK'S" at me in lime letters.

I toured the patio, with its empty pots – large and small – and its evergreen ones full of rosemary and holly. In one or two others were the quite beautiful, frosted remains of stalks and flowers. Hydrangeas? Not my favourite flower, but so pretty when dead. I crossed the lawn and reached the wooden shed before realising I hadn't brought the pad and pen with me. After retracing my steps up to the patio, I was halfway through the sunroom when I heard Jamie saying, 'Fuck! Fuck!'

Had he burnt something already? So much for his skills.

'For Christ's sake,' said Zara in a screechy whisper, 'you could have killed them!'

I halted.

'They'd never have eaten it!' Jamie was whispering now, but noisily, desperately. 'Mum loathed mushrooms, and she made all the meal decisions.'

'Thank God she did.'

'What shall I do with it?'

I took a step back. Mushrooms? Could have killed…? What was I hearing?

'Bury it,' Zara snapped.

'OK, but where?'

'Not here, obviously. Jesus, Jamie, how could you have been so stupid?'

'I just forgot. Forgot I'd made two lots, just in case.'

'And that you'd stashed the second batch in Mum and Dad's freezer? What were you on, you fucking moron?'

Not only was my heart going like the clappers, but when I started to reverse back out to the safety of the garden, my legs lost strength and buckled, and the side table I bumped into wobbled and sent a metal ashtray onto the tiled floor. Luckily, it was empty.

'What was that?' said Zara.

'Fuck, it's Edie.'

'Shove it in the bin! Quick!'

'Do you think she heard? Shit.'

'I'll go and check.'

After putting the ashtray back with a trembling hand, I ran outside. At the far end of the patio I did a one-eighty, so I was facing the house, then flung myself down and lay half on the steps to the lawn and half on the patio tiles. I reached for a large floral pot, pulled it over and heard a crack.

'Aargh,' I cried out. 'Oow!'

Zara hurried towards me. 'Are you all right, Edie?'

I sat up, and grimaced and rubbed at my shoulder. 'I think so. Ouch. I was climbing the steps, tripped, and lost my balance. I seem to have broken this pot, sorry.'

She stood it upright. 'It's just chipped, and besides they're yours to take, remember?' She helped me up. 'Are you really OK?' She looked more concerned than suspicious.

'Not sure.' I took a few steps, limping. 'I was coming back to get the notepad. A touch of low blood sugar, I expect. That'll teach me not to skip breakfast!'

Zara was showing no signs of not believing me, and I relaxed, as much as I could in the vicinity of a murderer, or possibly two. At least I had a good reason to be shaking now, as Zara led me by the waist to the kitchen.

'I think Edie's in need of food,' she told Jamie. 'Had a dizzy spell and fell.'

'Oh, bad luck,' he said. 'Grub's almost ready, if you want to clean up?' He was looking at my clothes, which just needed a brush down.

'OK, cheers. No, no I can manage,' I told the hovering Zara.

I limped my way to the cloakroom, picking up my bag on the way. Having locked the door, I took out my phone to text Ben. I switched it on, but nothing happened. Not until an apple appeared, followed by instructions on how to set up my new iPhone.

No! screamed my head.

I rummaged through my bag but my real working mobile wasn't there. I'd picked up the wrong one. Jesus Emily, I'd been perfectly happy with my old phone.

I mulled over what to do. Say something had come up and leave? Say I felt unwell after the fall and leave? Yes, obviously that would be the best course of action. Get in the car, go home, phone Ben. I brushed dust and leaves off my clothes, splashed water on my face and went back to the kitchen, where Jamie was placing stews and veg on a tray.

'That was quick,' I told him.

'Microwaved.'

Zara said we'd eat next door since the kitchen table was loaded. She nodded towards the sunroom and asked what I'd like to drink.

It was no good, I couldn't leave now. 'Just water, thanks.'

'Yeah, I'd better stick to water too,' said Jamie, grinning at his sister.

She tutted. 'Well, I was very good last night, so I'm going to treat myself to Dad's gin.'

'Lush!' said Jamie.

'Any broken bones?' Zara asked as she handed me my water.

'No, no broken bones, but I'm sure there'll be bruises tomorrow.'

'You won't sue us, will you?' She laughed again.

Had I imagined hearing all that earlier? Or got the wrong end of the stick? 'Um, let me think,' I said, attempting to match their tone. 'Not if I can have the two filing cabinets, Jamie.'

We sat in bamboo armchairs in the sunroom, bowls of stew on our laps. There was a lot of chat between the siblings about household and personal items, and which of their drivers they'd use to transport everything. Zara had swiftly polished off her G & T and was on her second. It was the only sign that either of them might be rattled.

'Is the new owner going to continue with the storage and removals business?' I asked. I really wasn't interested, but my brain kept telling me to behave normally until I'd gathered the things I'd listed and bid Jamie and Zara a friendly farewell on the drive.

'Yes, thank the Lord. They've bought it as is, so we haven't had to flog the vans and so on. They're reemploying a lot of the staff too, so Mum and Dad aren't wracked with guilt.

Because I hadn't wanted to die, I'd only pretended to eat the food. Then, putting it to one side, I asked if I could make myself a tea, as I was still feeling shaky.

Jamie said yes and he'd like one too. 'Milk, one sugar. Cheers.'

'I'm fine,' said Zara, raising her glass.

In the kitchen, I put the kettle on and once it was noisy enough, I pressed the top of the bin and it sprang open. Nestled on top of all the rubbish sat a plastic container with what looked very much like frozen cream of mushroom soup inside. I quietly closed the lid, washed my hands thoroughly, and made two teas.

'There you go,' I said, placing Jamie's beside him. 'If it's OK with you guys, I'll take a quick look around the garden and shed?'

'Remember the pad and pen this time!' said Zara. 'Or list them on your phone?'

'Phone's playing up,' I told them.

I fetched the pad and pen I'd used before and took them and my tea across the patio – remembering to limp – then down three steps and over the lawn to the shed.

Once I was in, I propped myself against a shelf of tools and took one, two, three deep breaths. I was still shaking. Unsurprising, since I was in the company of killers with no means of communication. Looking around me, I wrote shears and secateurs, neither of which I'd need because

Astrid had pruned everything to an inch and left me with a lawn so small I could trim it with nail scissors.

I needed to get this over with, so puffing myself up, I went back into the house to show Zara my list. But Zara wasn't in the sunroom, or the kitchen, or anywhere downstairs. And neither was Jamie. I called upstairs but got no response. Odd. Were they out burying the evidence? If I was brave, I thought, I'd go and find out what they were up to and where, so that I could lead the police to the exact spot.

I went upstairs, just to check. Perhaps they were in the attic having a whispered chat. But as I passed a window on the first-floor landing, I spotted them. They were outside, having a conflab, over by the storage units, heads together. As far as I could tell, neither was holding the plastic container.

Next thing I knew, I was flying down the stairs and back into the kitchen. I opened the bin and saw the box. Still there, good. Or maybe bad. I looked around the kitchen and spotted a stack of similar freezer boxes on the table. In the fridge, I found a large tub of apricot yogurt, opened and definitely off.

I filled a box with it and put the lid firmly on. From a neat stack, I took two tea towels. Trembling and terrified, and cross that I couldn't take a photo as evidence, I lifted the box from the bin with one cloth, then wrapped it in the other. I placed the yogurt-filled container in the bin, closed the bin lid, and ran through the kitchen and down the hall with the soup. I picked up my bag, took my coat off the hook, tugged the car key from the pocket and went through the front door, closing it as quietly as I could close something that heavy.

Sprinting towards my car, I zapped it unlocked, then threw myself, bag, and coat in and placed the box on the passenger seat. I had a roll of large freezer bags in the glove compartment because Billy had said they were a handy addition to any car. 'You never know when you'll need to bag something mucky,' he'd said.

Or even lethal.

I popped the plastic box inside and placed it in the passenger footwell.

Having started the engine and aware that Zara and Jamie might hear it, I quickly reversed away, swivelling the steering wheel until I was facing the roadside entrance, then drove to the gate. Once on the road into Fellford, I put my foot down and ignored all speed cameras.

EIGHTEEN

My hands clammy on the steering wheel, my eyes constantly darting to the rear-view and wing mirrors, I took a convoluted route via Long Hanborough, just in case Zara or Jamie spotted the apricot yogurt and jumped in Jamie's car and were attempting to catch up with me at great speed. The more obvious route would have been along the A40 to the north of Oxford, although I could also have gone via Elmbridge to my house in the east of the city. Stupid me, I thought. If I'd taken that route, I could have let myself into Billy's place. Too late now.

Going home wasn't an option, and neither was going to Jessica's, Astrid's, or Emily's, and putting them at risk. There was the police station, of course, but Jamie and Zara might have been lying in wait, guessing I would go there. Ready to bundle me into their car and pour cold mushroom soup into me. I glanced at the wrapped container in the footwell and shuddered. I might as well have had a loaded gun in the car. A gun would be a preferable way to go, thinking about it.

When I came to a junction that said Woodstock to the left and Oxford to the right, I went left. I wracked my buzzing, jumbled brain, trying to come up with someone I knew in Woodst–

Oh shit. I did know someone. Greg.

Owing to the central location of his house, there were no empty spaces nearby, so I found a council car park and got a ticket from the machine. I stood for a while, waiting to see if a black car cruised by or into the car park, but all was quiet at five o'clock on New Year's Day, as you'd expect. The lack of human beings unsettled me, so I took the box from the car, checked around again and hotfooted it to Greg's, praying he'd be in.

He was.

'Edie! What a coincidence, I was just fantasising about you.'

Oh, Christ, why did he have to look so good. 'That's funny,' I said, 'because I never even think about you.'

'Come in.'

'Thanks.'

'I see you've brought Tupperware,' he said, kissing both my cheeks. 'Anything good in there?'

God, it was tempting. All that time putting up with his–

'Don't touch it!' I told his outstretched hand.

I stepped into a house I'd seen only once, when I'd delivered a box of things he'd left at my place. It had looked rough as hell back then, but now it was gorgeous.

We'd tried living together at mine for three months after he'd ended a rental and made an offer to buy an 18th-century doer-upper in Woodstock. 'If this living together works out,' he'd said, 'I'll rent out the Woodstock house.' He moved into it on the day the sale completed, and I suspected that had been the plan all along.

'I'm in a bit of a predicament,' I said, tucking the poisoned food behind the sofa, asking if I could wash my hands, then taking a seat at a rustic table that went with the exposed beams, flagstone floor and log fire. Like Billy's, it was all opened up downstairs. Unlike Billy's, it was small and way too cosy. The cottage was one of a row, close to the town centre and the grounds of Blenheim Palace. 'Before I start,' I said, remembering that animals will eat anything, 'you don't have a dog, do you?'

'No, why?'

'Oh, nothing.' I got up and checked through a slit in his off-white linen curtains, pulling one curtain back an inch, but seeing only blackness. I sat back down and watched Greg pour me a glass of red wine I hadn't asked for but suddenly craved. One would be fine. It would calm my jitters. 'I'll need to use your phone, but first I'll explain why I ended up here.' I gave him a potted version with no names.

'God, what an exciting life you're leading these days. Quite a turn on.'

'Oh, Greg,' I sighed. 'You like women aged twenty and size eight, so just stop with the flirting. I know you, remember? Now give me your phone.'

'I've changed,' he said quietly, and handed it over. 'I really have.'

I found the number and called Cowley Police Station, but Ben was out, so I asked the woman to get a message to DS Watson to call me. I gave her Greg's number and said it was urgent. Since I knew no one else's number, not even Billy's, I was in the position of having nothing to do but wait and drink the very fine wine in my hand.

That wasn't entirely true. I could have found Billy's mobile number via his website. I ran through the scenario. He'd be on his way home but would take my call on speaker, then pull over at the next opportunity. He'd ask where I was, and when I told him he'd ask why I'd gone to a much-derided ex-boyfriend's place and not his. I'd have to explain about the weird route I'd taken and… I really didn't want to call him.

While Greg was telling me about a relationship that had recently ended, he occasionally shook his head of brown waves and curls. It was longer than it used to be. Midlife crisis? I was pleased to see some grey there.

'Trouble is,' he said, giving me his adoring-spaniel look, 'I couldn't help but measure her against you, Edie. Same with the others. And the result was always the same.'

'I was found wanting?'

'No, silly. They were.' His eyes were downcast but then he went spaniel again. A spaniel with blue eyes. 'I'm serious. I guess I didn't appreciate what I had at the time.'

I waved a dismissive hand, as though I hadn't cried for the whole of June, July and August that year, then spent a fortune on therapies to help me recover. I'd considered sending him a bill. 'You were young. You still are, damn you.'

'I'll be forty-four next week.'

'Exactly.'

'And you? You're…'

'Forty-eight.'

'So forty-nine in July?'

'April.'

'Hurtling towards the big–'

'Yes, all right!'

'God, I've missed you.' He looked into my eyes. 'I honestly have. You turning up here is like a marvellous dream.'

I laughed, at length – adrenaline, wine – but then noticed he looked hurt. Good, I thought. About time.

* * *

'You'll be fine with another half a glass,' said Greg. We'd moved to the sofa, where I kicked off my shoes and leaned my head back into a velvety cushion.

'Go on, then,' I told him.

'This is like old times,' he said.

'It isn't. For a start, I'm living with someone.' I checked the kitchen clock. Why hadn't Ben called? Should I have stressed the urgency a bit more?

'Oh,' said Greg. 'Oh.' He took our two glasses back to the table and filled them both to the top.

Don't drink all that, I told myself. Just don't.

'How long?' he asked.

'We met in September.' I told him about my house improvements and Elmbridge, and how the toing and froing had got a bit tedious. I also told him about our one week at mine, one at his, and one apart schedule.

He put the glasses on the coffee table and sat too close. 'So, is this one of your apart weeks?'

I caught that nice familiar smell. Chemistry, I thought, the cause of so much trouble. 'It is,' I said quietly.

His fingers were tucking hair behind my ear. I conjured up Billy, or tried to, then before I knew it, we'd slipped back in time, his arm around my shoulder, my head on his chest. I was in shock, I told myself. Traumatised. No harm in accepting a little comfort. The sofa was soft, the fire was both warming and exciting.

'Have you missed me?' he asked.

'No.' Once I'd spent hundreds getting him out of my head and heart, I hadn't. Or perhaps time had done it for free. 'Maybe. Sometimes. I don't know…'

I looked up into Greg's oh-so-familiar eyes, and the world of Zara and Jamie and poisoned soup disappeared.

But then a bash of Greg's door knocker made us quickly pull apart and leap up.

'Are you expecting anyone?' I asked, the terror of my journey rushing back in.

'No.' He made a move towards the hallway.

'Hang on a sec,' I told him, then dived behind the sofa, picked up the soup in its bag, and ran upstairs with it. I rushed around, looking for a hiding place, then saw that Greg's bath had a sliding panel. I heard assorted voices downstairs, but not clearly. Neighbours, I hoped. Friends. The panel was stiff, but I opened it far enough to hide the box beyond the spray cleaners. Downstairs, Greg's phone rang and rang until it stopped. Damn, probably Ben.

Then I heard a loud thud, like something falling.

Oh, Jesus. I picked up the only weapon I could think of and ran to the top of the stairs.

Greg was lying completely still at the bottom, and the front door was closed. It had to be Zara and Jamie, but had they gone? No, I heard voices, then Jamie appeared and took the stairs two at a time towards me.

I screamed, aimed the nozzle, and sprayed bath cleaner in his face.

'Shit!' he said, an arm shooting up to his eyes. 'Bitch!' I watched him wobble and fall backwards.

Greg sat up just as Jamie tumbled beside him, then managed somehow to pin Jamie face down and get his scrawny wrists behind his back.

I raced to the bottom on shaky legs. 'Are you OK, Greg?'

'Yeah, kind of. We just need something to tie him with.'

I scanned the small hall. Two coats, a pair of shoes and a brolly. 'Are you wearing a belt?'

'Yep,' he puffed, still gripping Jamie's wrists. 'But you'll have to…'

'Right.' I knelt down and lifted his shirt while Jamie wriggled beneath him. Greg watched as I tugged at his belt buckle.

'I told you it was like old times,' he whispered.

'Very funny.'

'Where is it?' asked Zara, suddenly looming over us. 'Edie, what have you done with it?'

'Get them off me, Zar!' squealed Jamie. 'I'm fucking blind!'

Surely not, I hoped. I ripped the belt from Greg's trousers, and between us, we wrapped it around Jamie's wrists and led him through to the living room. If Zara had had any sense, she'd have left and caught a flight to a country that wouldn't extradite her. Instead, she sat at Greg's table and drank red wine directly from the bottle.

'Zara?' he pleaded. 'Do something.'

'My brother's an idiot.' She took another swig. 'Enough's enough, Jamie. I can't protect you from your stupidity any longer.'

I picked up Greg's phone and set it to record. 'What do you mean?'

'It was only supposed to make him ill,' said Jamie.

Greg lowered him onto a dining chair, arms tied behind him, then went and filled a large bowl with water. 'Here, dunk your face in it.' he said, and Jamie obliged, coughing and spluttering afterwards. Greg dabbed Jamie's face with a tea towel, went back for fresh water, and repeated the process. I knew an apology was required, but this wasn't the moment, not when I was acting tough. I noticed Greg rubbing his jaw and guessed Jamie had taken him by surprise with a punch.

'Make who ill?' I asked.

'Oh, come on, Edie.'

'He and Hugh fell out,' said Zara, 'over a woman.'

'Does she mean Lucy, Jamie?'

He nodded, which was no good for my recording. 'Sorry, who?'

'Yes! Lucy!' His eyes were extremely red.

'So, were Hugh and Lucy…?'

'How many fingers am I holding up?' asked Greg.

Jamie squinted. 'One?' When I gasped, he smirked. 'Just kidding. Four.'

'They were sleeping together,' said Zara.

Jamie sniffed and tried wiping his nose on his shoulder. 'Shagging my girlfriend, shagging my sister, all the while married to hot rich Jessica.'

I couldn't help wondering how Jamie knew Jessica was hot. Had they met, or had he just checked out her website?

'I forgave Lucy,' Jamie continued. 'She's young. But that bastard Hugh?' He had tears running down his face, or perhaps water.

'Are your eyes OK?' I asked.

'No. Really sore and itchy.'

'It's probably just lemon juice.' I went and got the bottle and read out its environmental credentials.

'Still stings like fuck.'

'I thought you'd killed Greg, so…'

'Listen,' said Zara. 'Edie.'

'Yes?'

'Please, please, you're the only one who knows. Obviously you overheard us in the kitchen.'

'I did.'

'But no one else need know.' She glanced at Greg. 'Apart from your friend. It's just that it really was an accident.'

'How do you know? Were you involved?'

'No, no. Jamie told me he'd only meant to teach Hugh a lesson. I mean, look at him, Edie. My little brother's not capable of committing murder.'

I did look. I saw someone who'd tried to steal a dead man's money and almost knocked out my ex-boyfriend. Oh, and who thought poisoning someone was a reasonable punishment for bedding his girlfriend.

'Tea, anyone?' asked Greg. He frowned and shook his head at me, meaning don't do what these crazies are asking.

'If you could just forget everything you've heard today?' Zara pleaded with me. 'Hugh's gone and nothing will bring him back. I loved him so much, and even I don't want to see the culprit go to prison. Not for something accidental. A prank gone wrong. Please, Edie.' She was crying and I felt for her.

I picked up the phone and stopped the recording, then while Greg popped a straw in Jamie's tea, I asked Zara how they'd known where I was.

'We followed you, of course. Lost you just before Woodstock, but then saw you being let into this house by, well, a very large man. We spent ages waiting for you to leave, then thought fuck it.'

I looked at Greg. Not very large, I thought. Just right. But maybe in the doorway of a tiny cottage… I excused myself and went upstairs, where I called the last number to have rung Greg's phone. It had been Ben.

'I'm outside,' he said.

'Oh!' I pulled back the bedroom curtain. 'Yeah, I can see you, just. How did you find me?'

'Traced the phone owner's name and address. Is everything OK?'

'It is now.'

'Thank God for that. I was just with Billy at your house. Neither of us could get hold of you and we were worried. Me especially. Copper's instinct. Shall I let him know you're with a friend and that he can go home?'

'Would you? Thanks. Oh, best not to tell him who.'

Ben paused before saying, 'No problem.'

'Tell him I'll ring him tomorrow. Listen, I've got Jamie and Zara here. Jamie might have something to tell you about Hugh's poisoning.'

'Ha! So it was Jamie that Andrew saw. I knew it.'

'Andrew?'

'Came into the station today. Used to be a groundsman at Warlop, but retired, travelled for several months, and has just come back. He heard about Hugh and said he'd seen a young blond chap visit Hugh in the lodge, carrying a flask of something. A day later, he found the cup of the flask in the grass and kept it.'

I went back to the sliding bath panel and took out the box and gave Ben a potted account of the overheard conversation and the recording I'd done. 'I'll unlock the front door. Zara's pretty upset, so you might not want to…'

'Come in guns blazing? Don't worry.'

I went down and got the key from Greg. 'Sorry,' I told Zara when Ben followed me into the room carrying the mushroom soup I'd just handed him. Jamie was then unbound and the front door was relocked.

'Right,' said Ben. He seemed weary. New Year was no doubt a busy time for the police. He took out a notepad and sat adjacent to Jamie and opposite Zara.

'In your own words, Jamie.'

'It was an accident.'

'What was?'

'Hugh's… death. He'd pissed me off and I wanted to make him suffer, like he made me and Lucy – well, maybe not Lucy – and Zara suffer. And Jessica, of course. So, knowing how much he liked mushroom soup, and also knowing where he was hiding, I decided to make him some.'

'Shouldn't he have a lawyer here?' asked Zara.

Ben sighed. 'Do you want one, Jamie? We'd have to do things more formally, at the station…'

He shook his head. 'I'm responsible, Zar, so what's the point?'

'OK, carry on,' said Ben.

'Anyway, my mother… our mother, is a keen gardener, isn't she, Zar?'

Zara nodded, crying again.

'And as kids, she'd always tell us never to touch the hydrangeas because they were poisonous.'

'Are they?' I asked.

'Apparently,' sniffed Zara. 'When we were young, Mum was always worried about berries and the like, so made a point of learning all the poisonous plants. Lilly of the Valley was one, I remember.'

Ben tapped his pen on his pad. 'Carry on, Jamie.'

'So, I picked one or two hydrangea leaves and petals, finely chopped them, and added like just a sprinkle to the soup. It was hardly anything. Like I said to Edie, I just wanted to shake him up a bit. I read that it can make you nauseous, dizzy… give you a bad tummy. Nowhere did I read that it could take out a fully grown man. A rabbit, maybe, if it had too much.'

Ben looked at me. I looked at Ben. Hydrangea?

'I'd made quite a lot of soup, so I divided it in two. Put one half in a flask and hid the other half, just in case it didn't work the first time.' He nodded at the box Ben had put on top of the fridge. 'That's what's in there.'

'Idiot,' said Zara. 'If you hadn't kept it, we wouldn't be here.'

'Did you add any other poisonous items to the soup?' asked Ben, laying down his pen. 'Obviously, we will be examining it.'

'Like what? Death cap mushroom? No.'

'And where was Hugh when you took it to him?'

'Living in Hilltop Woods, in a kind of brick hut thing. He'd flagged me down in my car one day, a week or so before, just outside Fellford. Wanted a chat. Afterwards, I dropped him off at the entrance to the wood. I followed him on foot, but he didn't know.'

'What was the chat about?'

'He didn't have a phone, he told me, which was why he waited for me to drive by. He wanted me to get him a smartphone, with a sim-only contract in someone else's name. He said he was hiding from Jessica so she couldn't divorce him. Tried to convince me he hadn't touched Lucy – that he'd never do that to a mate. You effing arsehole, I wanted to say because Lucy had already owned up. But I was being Mr Nice. Gave him a bit of money. Then he asked me if I'd go and get some cash he'd hidden in their Oxford flat, in some encyclopaedias no one ever read. He was in a state, but I couldn't feel pity, just contempt. After that I hatched my plan.'

'So you didn't go into the place he was staying in?'

'No. When I went back a week later, as arranged, I met him at the gate at twelve on the dot, and we went for a walk. He thought I'd have the money, but I told him there'd not been an opportunity yet and that I'd forgotten to buy him a phone. I hadn't forgotten. One, I couldn't be arsed to, and two, I didn't want him calling Lucy. He wasn't happy but I slipped him more cash to calm him down. We sat in a nearby field and he drank the soup and ate the roll I'd brought along. I told him I'd had lunch at the café and wasn't hungry.'

'And what date did you take the soup to him?'

'August, 26th.'

'You seem sure of that?'

'Yeah, it's my mate's birthday. Went to his later that day to celebrate.'

'Could you describe the thermos flask?'

'Er, you know, just the usual. Stainless steel.'

'The cup too? Was that stainless steel?'

'Yeah, why?'

Ben stood up. 'Excuse me, I just need to make a couple of phone calls.' He pointed at the back door. 'May I?'

Greg went and unlocked it. However he'd thought his day might unfold, it probably didn't look like this.

Ben was gone for a good twenty minutes, during which time Zara used the loo, Greg opened a new bottle of wine and poured himself a glass, and I used his phone to look up hydrangeas. I thought of the pretty frosted ones on the Peacocks' patio. Turned out lots of our most loved flowers and plants are toxic when eaten. Who knew?

'Did you give Hugh anything else that day?' Ben asked Jamie when he returned.

'Like?'

'Magic mushrooms?'

Jamie shook his head. 'Nope.'

Ben was quiet for a while, tapping his pen again. 'Listen, Jamie, I'm going to have to take you to the station to make a proper statement, but if you are telling the truth, it's highly unlikely you were responsible for Hugh's death.'

Zara made a strangled sobbing noise, and Jamie said, 'You're joking?'

'One last thing. No, two. Have you still got the flask?'

'Yeah, gave it a good wash though, in the dishwasher.'

'What?' cried Zara.

'Not at the café, in Mum and Dad's. Don't scream, it was the only thing in there, and I ran the machine with that cleaner stuff after.'

'And you've got the whole thing, have you?' asked Ben. 'The top too? The cup?'

'Of course.'

'Secondly, did you tell anyone what you'd done, or were planning to do?'

'No,' said Jamie, frowning, eyes zigging left and right. 'Hang on… Er no. Or maybe… Did I? No, no. I mean, that would have been seriously dumb of me.'

NINETEEN

What was wrong with me? I'd had a happy childhood, hadn't I? Yes, adulthood had got off to a rocky start, and while a single mum I'd been messed around by one or two boyfriends. But that didn't explain why I was in Greg's bed at four in the morning with only a dim recollection of how I'd got there. I appeared to be fully clothed apart from socks and shoes, so presumably, I hadn't crossed that line.

My brain was hacking its way out of my skull, so I got up and went in search of painkillers. I found them in the kitchen, and while I was there I slipped on Greg's garden crocs. Stone floors are lovely, but not in the night when the fire's practically out.

I made a cup of tea and sat at the table, looking at the last embers of the ashy logs and going over the Hugh business.

After failing to bump off Hugh, had Jamie gone back with something stronger? Death cap, for example. Or had he owned up to his sister and she'd gone back with something stronger? It really had been too much of a coincidence, Jamie's mildly poisoning Hugh, but not enough to kill him – according to some expert Ben had talked to in the garden – then Hugh actually being poisoned soon after, by his own or another's hand. Plus, it was possible that a thermos flask was used both times. There had to be something linking the two events.

Ben had called me on Greg's phone mid-evening and told me more about his interview with Andrew, the groundsman. Although Andrew initially said he'd found the flask top the day after seeing Jamie at the gate, he'd suddenly remembered it had been three days after. He'd gone to say a final farewell to the woods at around two.

'Poor chap was gutted,' Ben had added. 'Not used to making errors like that. He told me all about his father's dementia. Bit of a talker.'

That new information meant there had been two days when someone else could have fed Hugh poisoned mushroom soup or slipped a dodgy mushroom in with his magic ones. The flask top Andrew had found was with forensics, and Ben had requested priority DNA testing.

'If there's no match, will Jamie be charged with anything?' I'd asked.

'Maybe assault. He did attempt to poison Hugh. We're keeping him in custody, just in case he confesses to going back to Hugh with death caps.'

It seemed unlikely to me, sitting there in a daze at my ex-partner's table, that there'd be any real development in the investigation into Hugh's death. But who knew?

Each time Billy popped into my head, I wrenched my thoughts back to Jamie and Zara and Hugh. But I could only keep that up for so long. Why had seeing Greg filled me with excitement and longing? It was so annoying.

* * *

Around midday, Ben called me on Greg's phone while Greg and I were walking around the Blenheim estate. Once again, Ben didn't comment on my location, situation, or general morals. I'd been trying not to think about my last walk there with Maeve's father, when the call came through.

'Bad news, I'm afraid.'

'Oh?'

'First, no prints – apart from Andrew's – DNA, or any traces of soup or anything were found on the flask cup.'

'That's odd.'

'It was, until I called Andrew and told him. It was then that he recalled taking it to the "bothy", as he calls it, to see if it was Hugh's friend's – the one he'd seen two days before. Hugh was out, so Andrew went in, looked around for the rest of the flask, couldn't see it, so decided to take the cup home, where he gave it a wee rinse.'

'Ah.'

'As much as I'd love to get a conviction for this one, there's not enough evidence to lead us anywhere. We've come across no signs or traces of death cap in any of the searches.'

'Oh well,' I said, and I thanked him for the call, then updated Greg.

'I don't know why I'm teaching undergraduates,' he said. 'Your line of work sounds far more interesting.'

I could have told Greg why he was teaching undergraduates.

Before leaving Woodstock, I found Jessica's number online and called her to bring her up to date. She was in London getting her house ready for tenants.

'That's so odd,' she said, 'and a little suspicious, don't you think? I mean, Jamie could so easily have gone back or got someone to go back and do the job properly. His sister, for example?'

'I don't know,' I said, recalling Zara's distress. 'I suspect she'd have owned up to it to save her little brother.' Or had Zara just been playing a clever game? 'The thing is, the police have nothing concrete. No standout suspect and no evidence.'

Jessica sighed into the phone. 'And no obvious motive, I guess?'

'Nope.'

'I kind of wish this hadn't happened,' she said, her voice cracking. 'I know you had to act when you overheard Zara and Jamie, but it's brought it all back, and… well, on top of the move out of this house, with all its memories.' She sniffed. 'Sorry.' I heard her blow her nose and then she was back. 'Not your fault.'

'Do you need a hand down there?'

'No, no. But thanks. I'm waiting for the agents to come and do an inventory, read the meters, etc., then after I've checked behind the radiators for knickers, I'm out of here.'

I laughed. 'I'll remember to do that if I ever move. Let's go for a drink when you're back?'

'Absolutely.'

In the car park, I got a bear hug from Greg. 'That was the nicest twenty-four hours I've had in a long time. Worth the punch in the face.'

I eased out of his grip and thanked him.

'What for?' he asked.

'Being home. Dealing with Jamie. All the tea and wine.'

'And dinner?' He'd fried a couple of pork chops with onions and heated oven chips. Billy disapproved of oven chips. I'd been trying not to make comparisons, but Greg's meal had been delish.

'And dinner.' I got in the car, started the engine and lowered my window.

'Can we…' he asked, bending down to my level.

'I don't know,' I said, not wanting him to think he'd been used, which was hilarious considering our history.

After pulling away, I watched him wave until I turned into the street.

* * *

Astrid came to the door dressed all in white, down to the pumps on her feet.

'Very virginal,' I said as she kindly let me in.

'You look like shit, Edie'.

I beamed. 'But I don't feel it, even if I should.'

'Shed?' she asked.

It was beautifully warm in there, with its convector heater. I took off my coat and scarf and hung them on the hooks. Astrid was soon at work with two Rizla papers, rolling them in a quick, deft way I'd never mastered. She handed me one, then took the other chair, lit up, passed me the lighter and said, 'So, you've had some kind of encounter with someone other than Billy and it's made you all gooey?'

'Shit, Astrid. How did you know it wasn't Billy?'

'Ha! Someone new, or Greg?'

I coughed and spluttered. 'Are you tracking my car?'

Astrid punched the air. 'Finally!'

'Finally what?'

'You're back.'

'Oh?' I said. 'Where did I go?'

'I've been calling it Billyworld. In my head, that is. I'm not a gossip.'

She wasn't, it was true. 'Sounds like Butlins.'

'But less fun.'

I took a long drag. 'You're implying that I've done that thing again, of meeting someone and getting subsumed by their preferences and tastes?'

'Don't forget interests.'

I leaned back and closed my eyes, feeling the strange effects of the smoke. 'No, Astrid. No, no, no. It's been fifty-fifty on the compromise front. Honestly.'

'Has it really? When did you last jump in the car on a whim and drive to Brighton?'

'Um, late August?'

'When did you last eat meat? Not counting yesterday.' Astrid laughed, which she didn't do often. 'Your face, Edie! That was a wild guess.'

'Pork chop. Delicious.' But wait, hadn't Greg ended up eating mine because all I could see was dead pig? I hoped I hadn't been rude.

'And when did we last do this?' She waved her spliff around. 'I'll tell you when, September.'

I looked at the thing in my hand. Was I enjoying it? No. Was I doing what Astrid accused me of, only with Astrid? I was.

'I'm not sure I want to smoke this stuff anymore, Astrid. Can you finish it?'

'Uh uh, germs.'

I put it out. 'What do I do?' I asked her.

'Were you and Greg intimate?'

'Sex? No. I stayed the night, though. Just got back. It was a dramatic day and I needed somewhere to hide. Long story. Anyway, my car just sort of took itself to Woodstock.'

'How clever.'

'Then, later, I'd had too much to drink to drive… and besides…'

'You didn't want to leave.'

'I didn't.'

'Where are you and Billy in the schedule?'

'I go to his in six days.' With her love of order, Astrid, unlike others, had never mocked our timetable.

'Well, you've done nothing wrong, so have a think about things and see how you feel in six days' time. Don't, whatever you do, go rushing over to Billy's and end things.'

'God, no, I couldn't do that. We have *Madame Butterfly*, a Wales rugby game and walking in the Pyrenees all booked.'

Astrid sighed and gave me a look.

'What?' I said.

TWENTY

At home, I picked up messages and voicemails and scrolled through missed calls. I put the new phone back in its box for when I had the strength to deal with it, then tried Billy. He didn't answer. I assumed that meant he was at work, rather than cross with me. I was right.

"I'll ring after five. Hope all's well xx", said the text I'd received many, many times.

I enjoyed an afternoon nap, deep and long, then woke to my phone ringing on low volume. It said 17.01 and Billy's name.

Heart heavy and filled with guilt, I let it ring out and stared at the ceiling, going over the previous day and reexperiencing the different emotions. First the relief, knowing I'd have not just the day but an entire week to myself. Next came cheerfulness as I drove to Fellford. Then the shock from overhearing Zara and Jamie, and the fear as I drove off with the soup. Relief again from finding Greg at home, followed by happiness and affection, then terror when Zara and Jamie arrived, and relief when Ben took them off to the station. Romance and nostalgia came when Greg cooked dinner, followed by drunken tiredness and sadness at having to leave him.

Now, getting up and straightening the duvet, I experienced only a serious case of butterflies. I went into the app that let Billy and I track each other's phones and changed the settings, then showered and dressed in the leggings and boots with a long cashmere jumper I'd forgotten I felt so good in. Before switching off the light, I peeked at Billy's pyjamas to see if they'd sway me. They were neatly folded beneath his three pillows. Sleeping semi upright is good for the heart, apparently. Not so good for spooning, I'd wanted to say. Instead, I'd added another pillow to my side because the uneven pillow heights unsettled him.

Minutes later, without resetting the alarm system Billy had bought me for Christmas, I jumped in my car and aimed for Woodstock, trying hard to feel like the bad and reckless person I clearly was.

I took the route through the city, rather than around it, as I wanted to stop for petrol at the end of Woodstock Road. Tootling along at thirty, I listened to Leonard Cohen, because I'd listened to so much of him with Greg. Was I doing that thing again, or just getting in the mood?

I was doing that thing again.

While I felt around the passenger seat for my phone, so I could choose a playlist of my own, a cyclist loomed out of a dark side street and almost into my path, causing me to swerve around them. Jesus, cyclists!

On reaching the service station, still shaken, I pulled into a parking space and sat for a while with the engine off and no music. Bike. Accident. Jessica. What had her mother been about to say about Jessica's accident? I hadn't managed to talk to her again, what with people drifting off and others turning up. Five hours of saying hello and goodbye, that's what hosting a party is.

I called Ben. 'Are you at work?'

'I am.'

'Don't suppose you have a number for Jessica's mum?'

'Hang on a minute. Er, yep, Andy spoke to her before I took over the case. Why?'

'Oh, um, she left something at my house, and I can't get hold of Jessica. A scarf. Also, I'd like to thank her for the housewarming present.'

'Is that right?' asked Ben, dubiously. 'What's going on?'

'Nothing. Look, I'll just try Jessica again.'

'I really shouldn't do this,' he said and texted it to me.

I hit the number and hoped she wasn't with Jessica. 'Hi, Christine,' I said cheerily, 'It's Edie.'

'Oh, Edie, hello. This is a nice surprise. How are you?'

'Fine, fine. Recovered from yesterday. Are you back home now?'

'I am. I enjoyed the party a lot. Thank you. Just putting my feet up and watching the box.'

'Nice. Jessica gave me your number so I could thank you for coming and for the gift.'

'Oh, you're welcome, love.'

'I forgot to ask where you live?'

'I'm in Wheatley.' Not too far, good. 'I moved down from Essex in December. Jessica insisted. She's set me up in a lovely bungalow, thinking of my old age, no doubt!'

I told her that was a long way off. I was out and about, I said, and not far from Wheatley. 'Maybe I could pop in for a cuppa? It'll be nice chatting to a fellow once-young single mum.'

'Yes, do! I'll put the kettle on. I was going to have a crumpet, if you fancy one?'

'Yes, please,' I said, then memorised the address she gave me. I risked not getting petrol since it hadn't dropped to the danger zone, and I drove off in the direction of Wheatley a little too fast. There was nothing worse than a cold crumpet.

By the time I arrived, it was tepid, as was the mug of tea. Christine said not to worry and popped both in the microwave. 'Thirty seconds and they'll be lovely. We'll sit in the lounge, shall we? Nice and cosy with the gas fire.'

'Great.' I so wanted Christine to be my mum. She went to the fridge and pulled out a bottle of white. 'I'll pour two and you can decide if you want it after the tea.'

'I'm sure I will, thank you. I'll stop at one, though!'

We talked for a bit about having our daughters so young and people's reactions, and the friends we'd lost and the new friends we'd made at the nursery, then the school gates. In the hope of bringing us closer to the present, I asked why she'd chosen to live in Wheatley, not Oxford.

'Well,' said Christine, 'it's close to Jessica and the boys but not too close. And as my daughter pointed out, you get a bit more bang for your buck here.'

'That's true. It must be nice having you around for support, after all she's been through.'

'Yeah, she's not as tough as she comes across. Although what happened last year would unsettle anyone. A weaker person would have ended up hitting the bottle, or worse.'

'You mentioned her bike accident in the early summer? Jessica told me about it, and how she suspected…' I was taking a punt and held my breath.

'Ah, so you know.' Christine sat back in her armchair. It was part of a suite I'd guarantee Jessica hadn't picked.

'Only that she…'

'That she knew it was him on the motorbike that charged into her as she cycled past with no working brakes, so she was going at a rate of knots. Jessica loved her Dutch bike, as she called it. Got it serviced at Wheels on Fire every spring and cycled around Oxford when the weather permitted.' Christine stared at the rag rug in front of the fire, then looked up at me. 'Those brakes were tampered with, and she knew it.'

'Yes.' I nodded knowingly, my heart suddenly racing.

'And of course, then she recognised him when he lifted the visor a little before roaring off. No witnesses, can you believe it?'

'No,' I said. 'On the other hand, it is a side street, and they are mainly busy during rush hours.'

My head tried to absorb. Hugh knocked Jessica off her bike and rode off?

'I always liked Hugh. There was the age gap, that was worrying, but once he really committed to Jessica, he was a good husband and a wonderful stepfather. The boys had such fun with him.' She gave me a quick smile. 'But they'll be fine. He's gone now, thank goodness, and they need never know what a truly evil person he was, not to mention reckless. Poisoned himself, the fool. What was the coroner's verdict, misadventure?' She picked up my wine from the coffee table and drank some. 'Oh, crikey,' she said. 'Sorry! I'll get you another one.'

'No, no. Still got my tea.'

'Did Jessica tell you she heard him willing her to die while she was in a coma? Thought he was praying for her at first. "Please, Jessica, please," he whispered in her ear. Then added, "Just fucking die."'

I somehow remained outwardly calm. 'Mm,' I said. It felt less like lying than a yes. 'But did Jessica ever tell Hugh she knew he'd knocked her off her bike, or that she'd heard him say that?'

'Good grief, no. I was a bit dubious about her claims at first, I'm afraid. Remember, he was extremely charming, and in recent years came across as the perfect husband and stepdad. Once he'd grown up, you know? And Jessica had been in both a nasty accident involving a head injury and a coma. I honestly thought she'd imagined it.'

'That's an understandable reaction, but then you changed your mind about him?'

'I helped out, you see, after she was discharged. Cooked and ferried the boys around and did a spot of cleaning, so I was in their house a lot. I'm no psychologist, but I couldn't help pick up on his lack of empathy. His frustration with her and his situation. Never with the boys, I have to say, just with the wife he hadn't successfully got rid of. And Jessica had told me about his girlfriend, Zara. I'd hear him on the phone to her, all romantic and promising they'd be together soon.'

'But if Jessica knew Hugh had tried to kill her, why didn't she go to the police?'

Christine knocked back more wine. 'Think about it, Edie. She had no proof, no witnesses to any of it, and even the tampered-with bike had disappeared. Hugh would no doubt have said she was suffering from mental illness following head trauma. He could be very persuasive.'

'Makes sense.'

'Also, Jessica believed even Hugh wasn't foolhardy enough to make a second attempt on her life.' Christine inched towards the front of her chair and leaned in. 'I had a bit of a word with Hugh myself. Told him how suspicious it would look should another accident befall his wife. Went as white as a sheet, he did.'

'Good for you, Christine. Perhaps you had a hand in him eventually leaving?'

'I like to think so. He took a lot of her things, you know. Expensive items, some with sentimental value. Bastard. Best thing that ever happened to her, though, him going. When it was obvious he wasn't coming back, she felt able to start divorce proceedings.'

'But then she couldn't locate him, so came to us for help.'

'My suggestion, actually. I found you online.'

'Oh, right.' That differed from Jessica's story. 'Thank you.'

'She was prepared to up the settlement to a hundred thousand, just to make sure he'd sod off and never try anything again. But he didn't get to hear about the increase because he had a misadventure in the woods with some funny mushrooms. A horrible way to go, but I can't feel sorry for him.'

'And Jessica never saw Hugh again after he moved out?'

'She didn't.'

Christine offered me more wine, since she'd drunk mine, but I declined and said it had been lovely chatting, only I should really go home and Skype Australia. I told her about my mother and sister, then she told me about her family, and in the end I did have the glass of wine while Christine told me about her ascendency to deputy manager at the bank, and I listed the pros and cons of teaching. Then finally, an hour later, after a nice mumsie hug from Christine, I got in my car and, feeling quite sick, called Ben.

'Have you still got Jamie?' I asked.

He hadn't.

'Oh. Any chance you could call and ask him if he saw Jessica at any point and divulged Hugh's hideaway and what he planned to do to him, or had done?'

'I can try. But I get the impression he hits the booze and drugs quite hard and has memory gaps.'

'Still, it might be worth asking.'

'Why?'

I gave him a summary of my chat with poor innocent Christine. 'It's too much of a coincidence, Jamie attempting to poison him, then somebody doing the same thing a few days later. Jamie was pretty evasive when I asked if he'd ever met Jessica, then hesitant when you asked if he'd told anyone his plan.'

'Yeah, I remember. Jessica certainly had a motive, and the fact that she kept the attempt on her life secret is a tad suspicious.'

'It is. And by reporting his disappearance to us, then telling the police she'd done that, she could have been covering herself.'

'Where is she now?' asked Ben. 'Do you know?'

'On her way back from London, at a guess. She's been doing a final clear up before letting her house.'

'OK. I'll talk to Jamie. Find out if he spoke to her about the great hydrangea plot.'

'Let me know what he says?'

'I will.'

After ending the call with Ben, outside Christine's, I saw I'd missed another one from Billy. He'd left a voicemail, but I chose not to listen to it. Later, I decided. In fact, tomorrow. It was our week apart, after all.

I had my hand on the car key, ready to turn it, when someone pulled up behind me, their lights dazzling in my rear-view mirror. When they dimmed, out got Jessica and my stomach knotted up.

Quickly adjusting the mirror, I slid down in my seat, stretching my neck to watch her. Once she was inside, I'd shoot off. But Jessica didn't go up the path to the bungalow. Instead, she took something from the back seat, then crossed the road to the area of grass and trees opposite.

I sat up and twisted my head to see where she was going, but before I knew it, she'd disappeared into the darkness. I called Ben to let him know what I'd seen, and he told me pretty bluntly not to leave the car under any circumstances.

'Does it look like she's hiding something?' he asked.

'Kind of.'

Ben sighed. 'Listen, we could be wrong about Jessica. On the other hand, we could be right. Don't move. Not right now.'

I had no desire to and told him so, not if Jessica was about to hear what her mother had told me.

'When it's safe,' he added, 'drive away. Like now, if she really is out of sight. Go home. We've got this, OK?'

The rap on the window an inch from my ear made me jump, freeze, half scream, and drop my phone. It landed upside down in my lap, and I heard Ben calling, 'Edie?'

I quickly pressed the off button, then pulled myself up and lowered the window.

'Hey,' I said. 'That's bad timing. I've enjoyed a lovely chat with your mum, but I've just arranged to meet Billy in town.'

'But isn't it your week apart?' She smiled broadly and opened my door. 'Come on, Edie. Give the guy a break. Let's crack open the bubbly I've been keeping for this day.'

'Oh, I've already had wine. Your mum, you know, very persuasive, ha ha.'

Could she tell I didn't sound anything like me? I certainly could. Ben would be on his way, I told myself, siren blasting and lights flashing. How quickly he was going to get here. I'd be fine, just fine.

'OK, maybe a wee drop. I'll text Billy.'

'Excellent!' said Jessica, and having left the safety of my car, I followed her up the crazy paving and once again greeted Christine.

Jessica kissed her mum, then put an arm around her waist. 'Look who I found outside,' she said, the two of them now facing me; Jessica's white-knuckled hand clutching Christine's cardigan. 'Mum called me just as I reached Wheatley, worried that she'd said too much. I got her to say exactly what she'd told you. Then I put my foot down, and as luck would have it, you hadn't yet left.'

'What do you mean?' I asked. 'We chatted about all sorts of things, didn't we, Christine? Being single mums, our jobs…'

Christine stood rigid, her face flushed. 'I thought she knew, Jess.'

'Oh, Mum,' said Jessica. 'You really, really shouldn't drink. Do you remember letting Hugh know I'd seen him at the accident scene? You'd been drinking then, too.'

'I know. I'm sorry, love.'

I worked hard at normal, but knew I wasn't pulling it off. 'Actually, I've just popped back to use your loo, if that's all right, Christine. Then I really must be off.'

'To Skype your mother? Yes, of course. You know where the cloakroom is.'

'Thanks,' I said, setting off down the hall and hearing a key firmly clicking the front door locked.

Don't be sick, don't be sick, my head repeated. Not on Christine's fitted cream carpet.

Once in the cloakroom, I slid the lock into place, took two steps to the window, and opened it. Before Christmas, I might have just made it through, but now… I got my phone out to text Ben, as speaking would have been risky. I'd put it on silent while chatting with Christine, so hadn't heard his four missed calls. "With J at C's", I typed. "She knows I know".

'I've poured you a small glass, Edie!' came Jessica's terrifying voice. She was on the other side of the door.

I flushed the loo and turned on a tap. 'Thanks! With you in a tick!'

Don't cry, please don't cry.

I sent another text to Ben, saying "Hurry".

Once again, I inspected the window. No, no way.

In the kitchen I was handed a full champagne glass. 'Mum's gone to bed,' Jessica said, and my nausea returned. Having Christine around had made me feel safe.

'To a new life in Oxford,' said Jessica, raising her glass, and doing the cheers-eye-contact thing.

'Your new life in Oxford,' I said, hearing the wobble in my voice and lifting my glass. Was the back door beyond Jessica unlocked? We clinked glasses, and I was about to drink, when something – or someone – said, 'Don't!' Hugh perhaps… Or my dad.

Jessica took two, three sips and said, 'Mmm, delicious.' She dabbed her lips with a finger and put her glass down. 'You're not drinking, Edie?' she asked, moving even closer. She took my glass and held it to my lips. 'Open, Edie!' she sang, then she stood back and laughed.

She was using my name too often, like psychopaths do. I attempted a chuckle, but heard a high-pitched cackle come out. I boldly took a large sip, then another. Did it taste bitter? Perhaps champagne always did. It had never been my favourite tipple, so I was no expert.

'Christine!' I called out. The bungalow's master bedroom was across the hall and down a little. I'd had a nose around on my way to the cloakroom, what now felt like ten hours ago. 'You're missing the champers!'

'Oh, Mum's out for the count,' Jessica said, 'once her head hits the pillow. Sadly, I didn't inherit that gene.' She tugged something from the pocket of her fitted denim jacket. I briefly wondered if I could pull off a denim jacket.

156

It was funny what pops into your head when you have minutes to live.

'I have to rely on these things.' She dropped a small box beside my glass. It had "Zopiclone" written on it, "7.5 mg". 'Hypnotics, basically.' She looked in the direction of her mother, one side of her mouth curled up.

Had Jessica spiked my drink? If she could do that to her already intoxicated mother…

'That was lovely,' I said. 'Thanks, Jessica. Now I really should–'

'Actually, no. You shouldn't. Not till you've heard me out.'

I spotted the wooden block of knives by the cooker, and Jessica followed my gaze.

'Oh, for goodness sake, Edie.' She went over to the knives, picked up the block and put it outside the back door. I could have run at that point, but where? Jessica locked the door and pocketed the key. 'All the windows have locks, in case you were wondering. Except the one in the cloakroom. But you knew that, didn't you, Edie? Thought you might be able to squeeze through?' She looked me up and down and laughed. 'Only Mum's cat has ever managed that. Her late cat. He and I didn't take to each other, sadly. Then shortly after Mum moved here, he became sick. The vet thought he might have eaten something bad out in the fields.'

I felt faint. Could this person I'd been looking forward to more fun nights out with – drinking, quizzing, giving the late-middle-aged oglers marks out of ten – be a serial poisoner?

'Look,' I said. 'Jessica. I don't understand what's going on here, and whatever your mum said made no sense. I just thought she was tiddly. I'm not sure what you think I know, but I assure you it's nothing.'

Jessica smirked. 'Nice try, Edie. Now give me your phone.'

'Why?'

A coldness crossed her face. 'How about because I asked you to?' She held out her upturned palm. 'How are you feeling, by the way?'

'Er, confused? Bewildered?'

'Confused and bewildered is good, Edie. Excellent, in fact.'

'I honestly wouldn't say anything, not to anyone, about this evening. Your mum burbling.'

When she wiggled the fingers of her outstretched hand, I sighed, defeated. I took the phone from my pocket and meekly handed it to her. People who've almost drowned claim that, after a while – after the terror and struggle – they reached a point of calmness and serenity. I'd never believed it until now.

'I just need your full attention for a while,' said Jessica. 'That's all. Let's go and sit in the conservatory and I can tell you the whole story.'

'OK,' I said. Everything would be OK. Just fine. It had somehow begun to feel like a dream, or a film. Like it was all happening to someone else.

The conservatory had vertical blinds, firmly closed, and a brown tiled floor that would be easy to clean blood off. It was cold in there, or I was, even in my coat. When Jessica launched into her version of events, I tried hard to follow.

'I just want to tell you what actually…'

My eyelids grew heavier as I caught most, if not all, of what she was saying.

'…was Jamie who gave me the idea … popped into my flat, completely stoned … something Hugh had told him … hidden cash. He didn't tell me where. Knew where Hugh was hiding … woods. Toby, Hugh's friend over the road … magic mush … I made Hugh's favourite soup … drove … talked Hugh into accepting a new settlement fig … no death cap … no way … and now there's no way of proving … since Andrew washed–'

Bang!

An explosion filled the conservatory, glass shattered, and all went dark.

TWENTY-ONE

Light was making its way through floral curtains. On top of me was a soft throw, and beside me was Christine, gently snoring. As I lay there, thick-headed and groggy, I tried to recall the events of the previous evening. Chatting with Christine, drinking champagne, a loud bang.

On the bedside table was my phone. I picked it up and saw several missed calls and messages, the last message being from Ben. "Morning", it said, "don't freak out when you wake up on Christine's bed. We have Jessica here at the station. There's a family liaison officer in the living room, ready to make you breakfast. Call me when the drug has worn off. Ben"

When I walked into the kitchen, a woman got up from the dining table and introduced herself as Amira. She asked if I'd like tea, coffee, or orange juice, and I went for coffee.

'Strong would be good,' I said.

'I heard you moving around so made some toast. Would you like eggs and bacon, too?'

'Yes, please.' When had I last eaten?

I followed her to the kitchen and propped myself on a stool at the breakfast bar. 'I think I remember an explosion?'

'Ah.' Amira smiled. She was very beautiful, and very young. She peeled streaky bacon from a packet and put four slices in a frying pan, then turned back to me. 'That was Detective Sergeant Watson and his team breaking into the conservatory. Bit of a mess, but we'll arrange for repairs. How do you like your eggs?'

'Fried? Not too runny?'

'Got it.'

'Thank you. This is very kind of you.'

'You're welcome.' She opened the fridge and took out the milk. 'There are some mushroo–'

'No! Thank you.'

Amira laughed. 'I do know a little about the case.'

'You wouldn't be able to give me an update?'

'I'm afraid not, but I'm sure the detective sergeant will notify you of developments. Milk and sugar?'

'Just milk, thanks.' I'd give Ben a call when the mental fog had cleared. 'Have I got time for a quick shower?'

'The house was searched last night, so yes, help yourself. Breakfast in ten?'

'Perfect.'

I looked in on Christine and saw she was breathing, then picked up my boots and coat and closed the door behind me. When I stripped off in the bathroom, I was surprised, to say the least, to see cotton wool and a plaster in the crook of my right arm. I'd had blood taken?

* * *

'Fuck me,' said Mike after I'd told them what had happened at Christine's. 'But I have to say, you look remarkably good, considering the ordeal you went through. Radiant, even.'

'Thanks.' I hadn't slept so well for yonks. But was I radiant because of Greg? I hoped not.

'Perhaps you're more of an adrenaline junky than you appear.'

Emily had her distressed face on. 'I'm sooo sorry we gave you a new phone, Edie.'

'Don't be daft, I love it. Well, I will.'

'Let me come round and set it up?'

'Would you?'

'Course.'

'So,' said Mike. 'What did Ben have to say earlier?'

'OK, so Jessica admitted to finding out from loose-lipped Jamie exactly where Hugh was in hiding and that she'd made some mushroom soup, put it in a flask, and taken it to him, just as Jamie had. No, she hadn't laced it with death cap. She said she loved her husband dearly, and just wanted him to come home.'

'Huh,' said Emily, tapping her chin with her phone. 'And what else did she say?'

'That she'd suffered from some mental impairment following the accident, and may have come out with some outrageous fantasies and imagined scenarios. She'd been on strong painkillers and had suffered with mental fog.'

Emily continued to tap. 'Yet she told her mum those things?'

'Quite,' said Mike. 'Who would frighten the life out of their mother, if they weren't sure?'

'I reckon,' said Emily, 'Jessica was dead sure she saw and heard him, and she passed it on to her mum, knowing she would say something to Hugh. Like she knew Christine got a bit chatty after a few drinks?'

'That's possible,' I said, and Mike agreed. He kept looking behind him at the clock. 'Do you need to be somewhere? I asked.

'Yeah, a tutorial in Botley. In half an hour.'

'OK, I'll speed up.'

'So,' Emily said, 'if Hugh knew Jessica suspected him of trying to bump her off, like literally… then Jessica's thinking was that he might not try again. Or if he did, he'd have had to, like, kill Christine too?'

I shuddered. 'Quite clever, really. What wasn't so clever was chucking the flask she'd used into the wooded area opposite her mum's house. The police found it, and it matches the top Andrew the groundsman found.'

Emily nodded. 'It's like once she thought the case wasn't going anywhere, she got a bit careless. Like she was clearing out her house and came across the flask, and chucked it in the car to get shot of it, only forgot, then realised when she got to her mum's.'

'I like it,' said Mike, putting things into his bag. 'What's puzzling, though, is if she had killed Hugh, why come to us to find him? Unless she just wanted to create a smokescreen.'

'That's what I reckon,' said Emily.

'Once again, quite clever,' I said. 'If risky.'

Mike stood up and swung the bag across himself. 'So what's next, Edie?'

'Unless Jessica confesses to adding death cap mushroom to the soup, or evidence is found that she did, then not much. The flask was washed, of course. Also, Toby is still refusing to talk, so even if he got hold of and sold the mushrooms, without him providing a name, they've run out of leads.'

Emily nodded. 'So it's all circumstantial evidence at the moment?'

'Yep.'

Mike headed for the door. 'I'll call you later, Edie. And well done, even though you should have phoned us to let us know what you were doing and where you were going.'

'Yeah, you should've,' said Emily after he'd gone. 'It's not like you're young… I mean—'

'No,' I agreed. 'It's not like I am.'

Emily and I went next door. Coffee for me and Coke for her, and two wraps. I asked how the move was coming along, and she said they were about to exchange contracts on Toby's flat so should be in by February.

'Me,' Emily said, 'owning a property in Oxford, can you believe it? I told Ben he didn't have to put me on the mortgage and deeds, but he insisted, what with it being all down to me that we got a nice place for such a good price. Toby's dad was worried about all the work we'd have to do, bless him, but we'll just take our time. Live in chaos for a bit, which might be quite romantic?'

'Will you get married?'

Emily blushed and patted her tummy. 'We might have to, if you know what I mean.'

'No!'

'I haven't told Ben I'm two days late, so not a word, Edie.'

'Just two days?' I said. 'So, you're not sure?'

'I am, yeah.' She beamed at me. 'It's a girl.'

'Emily, you can't possibly know that.'

She nodded. 'I do. Florence. Always loved that name. She looks like Ben. Well, not right now.'

I laughed. 'If you're right, you might have to speed up the flat renovation. Create a baby area.'

'Babies don't need much, do they? My gran, she said she slept in a drawer for months. Not that I'd want Florence doing that. I was gonna tell Ben last night, but then the Jessica thing happened.'

'Sorry.'

'Ha ha, don't be. I can't believe Jessica drugged you with *Zopiclone*. They gave me that at rehab, like a cosh to avoid the worst of the withdrawals. Why did she do that, anyway?'

'She told Ben she didn't want me shooting off until she'd explained what happened.'

'Will she get done for it?'

'I'd need to press charges it seems, but obviously I won't.'

'No,' said Emily. 'We don't want to get a reputation for taking our clients to court.'

'My thinking exactly.'

After leaving the café, I went home and slept for an hour or so, then had another shower and wondered what to do. I couldn't face Astrid, and I couldn't face talking to Maeve. What, I asked myself, did I really feel like doing? I sent a text and got a reply saying, "Of course x", then jumped in the car.

* * *

There was a space opposite Greg's house and I managed to squeeze into it. Night-time had arrived during the drive, and the cottage glowed enticingly through the downstairs window.

I'd missed a call, so checked it wasn't from Greg saying he'd had a better offer. It had been Billy, but this time, he hadn't left a second message. I remembered the previous day's and pressed play.

'Hi Eed, you OK? Noah and I are having a game of Monopoly, but it's not the same without you here, charging us rent for your Mayfair hotels. I expect you're sleeping off yesterday, but if you fancy a mac and cheese with smoked bacon, come and join us. Oh yeah, don't laugh, but my New Year's resolution is not to be totally vegan. See, that's how much I love you. Better go, Noah's looking through the Chance cards for a good one. Bye love.'

I looked over at the cottage, appalled. Greg? Really? Was I out of my mind? I listened to Billy again and smiled stupidly. Of course he mustn't eat animal products just for me. Did I even want to anymore?

I started the engine and did a three-point turn in the narrow street, almost bumping into Greg's cottage. On the way to Elmbridge with my 1980s playlist booming out of the speakers, I made my own New Year's resolution, which I'd begin implementing asap.

'Billy,' I rehearsed in my head, 'I do not want to go on an effing walking holiday in the Pyrenees in boiling hot July, OK?' He could take Noah to the Pyrenees, then he and I could go somewhere cooler, with crazy golf.

I stopped at the first garage I came across for petrol, now down in the red zone. "Love you too", I wrote before getting out. "On my way over xx".

Having managed to splash petrol on my hand, I put the nozzle back and pulled off a length of paper towel from a nearby roll. As I went to pop it in the litter bin by the shop, I stopped and stared at the bin, and stared at it some more, until a woman trying to enter said, 'Excuse me,' rather rudely. I apologised, paid for the petrol and drove over to the nearest parking space, where I texted Ben. "Just a thought but there's a compost bin in J's Divinity Road garden... bit of a long shot."

TWENTY-TWO

Five days later, as I pushed an empty trolley around Yarnton Garden Centre, I got a text from Ben.

"Bingo!" it said.

I should have felt pleased and proud, and maybe done a little jig, but instead my heart plummeted. All I could think about were the twins, first losing Hugh and now their mother.

But wait, had Ben been referring to something else? I called him and when it went to voicemail, left a message to ring me back.

Another aisle of shrubs greeted me. Some tall plants were needed in my front garden to act as a screen for the living room window, the previous shrubs having been destroyed by the builders.

I sighed. Plants, plants, plants... There were way too many to choose from and I started to lose enthusiasm for the project. Should I just stick with the Venetian blinds I had, even if they did reduce the light too much when fully lowered?

I wondered if they'd arrested Jessica.

No – a better idea – talk to Gary about switching from wood-effect blinds to white ones. They'd reflect the outdoor light. Perfect.

Surely Christine would step in to take care of the boys?

Or maybe off-white?

Plus they had their dad. And Pippa.

'Come on, Ben,' I whispered.

I abandoned my trolley to go for lunch in the garden centre's café, hoping they had a comforting soup. But before I got there, Ben called me back.

'Hi,' I said. 'Just tell me.' I sat on a rather nice patio sofa and held my breath.

'OK. The lab identified traces of death cap amongst the rotting compost. It takes very high temperatures to destroy the spores.'

'I remember.'

'So, we brought Jessica in last night and still have her. You're going to ask about the boys, aren't you?'

'Yes.'

'With their dad. He's come to Oxford.'

'Oh, that's good.'

'Jessica's claiming the compost bin was Hugh's idea and only he ever used it.'

'I'm not sure that's true,' I said, remembering the fresh veg I'd delved through that evening. How lucky I was to still be alive.

'No, it's bollocks. Want to know how we know?'

'Go on.'

'Newspapers.'

'Ah... hang on. Let me see if I can work this out.'

'OK, but quick. I'm a busy man.'

'I had a friend, way back, who'd shred the free newspapers for his compost. Said it sped up the process, or something.'

'So what—'

'Wait! Is this about dates?'

'Go to the top of the class, Edie. Jessica was most likely telling the truth about Hugh setting up the compost system. After he disappeared she carried on putting organic waste in there, presumably to cover the death cap even more. But what she wasn't adding to the mix was the occasional layer of newspaper, as Hugh had been doing.'

'And newspapers have dates on.'

'They do. We were able to determine that the scraps of death cap went into the bin after the last shreds of newspaper were added just before Hugh left Jessica.'

'Wow. But is it going to be enough to charge her?'

'That'll be up to the CPS. Obviously, we're pushing for a confession, but she's a tough cookie. Keeps saying anyone could have put it in the bin, even Hugh himself when she wasn't in Oxford. We've been talking to Toby's lawyer. See if we can come up with an enticement for him to own up to having had a part in it.'

'OK,' I said, surprised Ben was sharing this with me.

'I really do have to go, I'm afraid. I'll call you again later.'

'Yeah, do. And thanks, Ben.'

'No, thank *you*.'

In the café, I had soup. It was very tasty but didn't provide comfort. If it went to court, I'd probably be called as a witness to say Jessica had drugged me. Not a good look for a private investigator, and a horrible thing for the twins to hear.

I needed to talk to someone, but on the other hand, not really. The tension of having to shop for something home-related had now been wound up several hundred notches. What I wanted was to just be with someone and not necessarily talk.

Billy was at work. Also, we'd had words yesterday, about the proposed Pyrenees trip. All paid for and written in capitals on his wall calendar. Of course Billy had a wall calendar.

On top of that I'd left his kettle empty again, after making myself a tea. We'd not been speaking for a good hour, when I'd gathered my things and, right in front of him, written a note saying, "Bye".

I was just three miles from Woodstock, but would Greg be there? And even if he was, hadn't I closed that door? Maybe it was slightly ajar. No, I decided. Regardless of that narrow chink, Greg wasn't what I needed.

I could drive down to Brighton and have Maeve berate me for putting myself in danger again. Then there'd be the "I told you so" about Billy. No, too much like hard work.

After leaving the café, I wandered over to the food section, where – out of habit, and possibly guilt, and because we might be speaking again one day – I bought a jar of Billy's favourite chutney.

Next door in the antiques centre, I poked around the cornucopia of beautifully displayed items: old brooches, postcards, painted dressers, flags, sets of dining chairs, a naked mannequin. It was one of my favourite places, and so much more fun than shrub shopping.

But sadly, I felt too distracted to savour it all, and the idea of a long bath with a good book – but perhaps not a whodunnit – began to appeal.

I sped up my circular tour and was headed for the door when an attractive faded poster caught my eye. In the background was a mountain, rolling countryside and a tree. In the foreground was an old-fashioned globe. The capital letters at the top were very 1920s. "AUSTRALIA CALLS YOU" it said.

I stopped in my tracks. Mum, Jess, the dogs… still summer over there. Perfect.

If you enjoyed this book, please let others know by leaving a quick review on Amazon. Also, if you spot anything untoward in the paperback, get in touch. We strive for the best quality and appreciate reader feedback.

editor@thebookfolks.com

www.thebookfolks.com

Also in this series

THE MISSING AMERICAN (Book 1)

Edie Fox is more than a little suspicious when a wealthy American turns up to her cluttered backstreet office in Oxford, England, and hands her a bundle of cash to find his missing cousin. But not enough to turn down the deal. Yet she soon has more on her hands than she bargained for when an old flame enters her life, and the witnesses in her case start giving her the run-around.

FREE with Kindle Unlimited and available in paperback!

Other titles of interest

NO REFUGE
by Nicola Clifford

Reporter Stacey Logan has little to worry about other than the town flower festival when a man is shot dead. When she believes the police have got the wrong man, she does some snooping of her own. But will her desire for a scoop lead her to a place where there is no refuge?

FREE with Kindle Unlimited and available in paperback!

THE PIPER'S CHILDREN
by Iain Henn

A boy is found wandering in the woods, dressed in medieval clothes and speaking a strange language. When another child turns up, it doesn't shed any more light on the mystery for FBI agent Ilona Farris. Only by digging into her own past will she begin to work out what is going on, and who these children are, seemingly lost in time.

FREE with Kindle Unlimited and available in paperback!

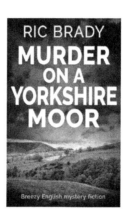

MURDER ON A YORKSHIRE MOOR
by Ric Brady

Ex-detective Henry Ward is settling awkwardly into
retirement in a quiet corner of Yorkshire when during a
walk on the moor he stumbles upon the body of a young
man. Suspecting foul play and somewhat relishing the
return to a bit of detective work, he resolves to find out
who killed him. But will the local force appreciate him
sticking his nose in?

FREE with Kindle Unlimited and available in paperback!

Sign up to our mailing list to find out about new releases and special offers!

www.thebookfolks.com